From Charmaine Gordon

There are four seasons:
winter, summer, spring, and fall.

And holidays: Christmas, Valentine's Day, Mother's and Father's Day, Fourth of July, Labor Day and Thanksgiving Day to name a few.

Where, oh where, is **Open Your Heart to Love Day?** There is no such day because love is there waiting to find all of us, no matter how old we are. Open your eyes and the doors to your closed heart. You are in for the ride of a lifetime you still have to live.

My name is *Charmaine Gordon,* a senior and the author of these Mature Romances. *Welcome to my world.*

The Beginning...Not the End

Volume 1

by

Charmaine Gordon

Vanilla Heart Publishing

The Beginning...Not the End
Volume 1

by Charmaine Gordon

Published by: Vanilla Heart Publishing

www.VanillaHeartBookAndAuthors.com

10121 Evergreen Way, 25-156

Everett, WA 98204 USA

ISBN-13: 978-0615888248   ISBN-10: 0615888240

10 9 8 7 6 5 4 3 2 1 First Edition

First Printing, October 2013
Printed in the United States of America

INSTANT GRANDPA

by

Charmaine Gordon

Dedication

Instant Grandpa is dedicated to the ones I love best: daughter Amy, grandest granddaughter Cassidy Rae, my youngest son Paul and my husband, Don. Thanks for your loving support as always.

Acknowledgements

Where would I be without the firm guiding wisdom of Kimberlee Williams? Thank you, Ms. K. for showing me the way. I couldn't ask for a better publisher, friend and editor rolled into one.

And to the Hudson Valley RWA, it's a pleasure being a member of this group of published authors.

A special shout out to the core Vanilla Heart Authors. We support one another and that's unique in this competitive world.

Chapter 1

"Who's taking care of you, little girl?" a deep male voice said.

I hurried across the hot sand where my granddaughter, age five, sat on a blanket smiling widely at a gray haired man with two little boys in tow. The small ice chest I carried bumped against my leg. *Ouch.* Guaranteed to leave yet another bruise on aging skin. Unless the stranger collected small kids for evil purpose, my little Patti seemed fine.

"Here's Granny. We're roomies. Mommy and Daddy are on vacation to Mexico."

Too much information to a stranger. I would have a little Granny chat with her soon about that.

"I'm Ralph Berg. These fine boys are my grandsons. Mike is four, Tony is six." He smiled. His white teeth gleamed against tan skin. The boys said hi and showed Patti their trucks and shovels.

"Hello, I'm Claire," and I busied myself with straightening the blanket, sun chairs and clamping the umbrellas. Alone with my granddaughter for the first time on vacation at the Jersey shore, I applied sunscreen to a wiggling Patti, tied her purple hat in place and wished this Ralph person would leave the boys to play and move on. *I'm a widow, for God sake. Can't he tell I'm in mourning from my black bathing suit?*

Years before, when beach front property at the Jersey Shore wasn't too expensive, I think dinosaurs roamed the earth back then, Larry and I bought our cute little house. With loving care, we renovated and winterized it to use all year. We raised a batch of kids and this is where we had the best of times. His ashes were inside a white stone bench near the house. My secret. The kids would not have approved. They kept telling me to begin again now that I'm single. *Single. The word didn't apply to me. After forty five years of marriage, I only knew about doubles.*

I sat down, stretched out and greased up with one eye on Patti who had playmates to keep her busy. And where did Ralph settle down? As if we had adjoining rooms, he set up camp next to me. The beach was crowded but really ... *not that crowded.* Lots of sandy real estate to spread out. I ignored him, removed pen and notebook from the old carryall and began to write a story lurking in the shadows of my mind.

A shipwreck with all passengers lost save one. A girl swims to shore. The wind blows her blond tresses dry as she strides on the sand, a trail of footprints in her wake. Her name is Claire.

Shrieks of laughter from the children broke my concentration. Ralph is up and running to check on them. *How nice.*

Rereading the few lines I'd written, I thought this sounds as if Shakespeare wrote it. *Twelfth Night? What in the world is going on?*

Chapter 2

Patti and I were together for ten days while daughter and her husband, what a good guy, went on a second honeymoon. The forecast might prove right this year with sunny days and no rain. I'd write the book my publisher waited for, at least get a good start, and Patti and I would have a lot of fun.

Except Ralph, the space invader, stood up, put a kite together and asked if I'd keep an eye on the kids while he made an attempt to fly his kite. "A maiden voyage, so to speak." He laughed a manly sound I hadn't heard for a long time.

I tucked my notebook away and figured I'd write after Patti went to sleep. Nothing like a hot date with my imagination as all writers know. "Sure, uh Ralph. I'm a great watcher. Good luck with your kite."

Why oh why did I encourage him with sparkling repartee? A simple yes would have been enough. As soon as Ralph left for the far end of the beach where other guys were flying kites, I struggled through the sand over to the kids with a great idea. "How about peanut butter and jelly sandwiches and juice?"

Patti jumped up out of the water hole they'd dug and grabbed the boys by their hands. "C'mon. My Granny makes the bestest sandwiches in the whole world."

Tony and Mike kicked up sand and stopped at our blanket. "Wow. Awesome." Mike inspected the chairs with umbrellas, ice chest and fancy blanket with corners you packed sand into daughter purchased when she brought the baby here.

Tony echoed his big brother. "Awesome, Granny. Can we sit down?"

Patti giggled. "Silly, of course you may." She pulled out wipes for their hands while I unwrapped sandwiches and opened juice boxes.

I warned them to be careful with their food. "Watch out for the sea gulls. They like to snitch your food."

Lunch turned out to be fun and I showed them how bread crusts were tossed to some aggressive sea gulls from a distance. A real trick. Then we all walked to the nearby public bathroom, took care of business and headed back to move our belongings before the tide came in. I glanced up at the far end where Ralph struggled with his kite. He needed a tail for his kite, I knew from years of experience. Already my mind went into homemaker mode. I'd have to make a tail and attach it for the poor guy. Men. I thought of Larry and realized I'd been so busy caring for someone else's grandchildren, I hadn't mourned too much today. *Hmm.*

The kids and I moved everything away from the rising tide and we decided to dig a deep hole and let the ocean fill it. Reapplying sunscreen to Patti , she said I should put some on the boys. I marveled at how quickly children became friends. They didn't take the measure of one another the way adults did.

I glanced up to see a dejected Ralph dragging his poor excuse for a kite behind him. Other colorful kites dotted the cloudless sky. Well I didn't intend for Mike and Tony's grandfather to be a loser. No way. Waving, I called to Ralph and he headed our way, shoulders slumped

Patti ran to him and held his hand. "Don't feel bad. My Granny knows how to fix kites. I bet she can make yours fly."

"Thanks, sweetie. I'm sure I can fix it myself. It's been a long time since I've tried. I think maybe when I was a young man."

"You're an old man like Grams is an old lady, right?"

"Patti, we are not old. We're just," I looked at Ralph, "a little bit older." She giggled and ran back to the boys. "We don't need munchkins to remind us, do we?"

Slowly he sank down on a worn beach towel, dropped the kite and groaned, holding his back.

I knew the signs. This called for cold water and all I had left in the ice chest were two juice boxes and two bananas. When Patti and I set out this morning, I didn't plan to be in the catering business. Ralph seemed inexperienced at taking care of his grandkids. I wondered about his background, wondered about a lot of things as my fingers expertly opened one juice box, stuck the damn straw where it belonged, took a sip so it wouldn't spill and handed it to Ralph.

"It's the best I can do on short notice and here's a banana. Good for potassium when you sweat on the beach or strain yourself."

He squinted up at me. "Thanks for your kindness to a stranger."

I wanted to say shut up and eat and drink. His eyes were green with flecks of brown. Hazel. "Where are you staying?"

He gestured up toward the dunes. "I rented the O'Brien's house. Do you know them?"

I laughed. "Grace and I bought around the same time. We've been friends ever since. I never rent my house."

"How come?" He peeled the banana and munched on it.

Why didn't I? So many reasons crowded my mind. I sighed. "Renting the house would be like giving my granddaughter away to strangers for a week. She's so precious and, well so is the house. We built it and the thought of

13

anyone living there ..." Tears threatened to fall so I turned my head and just in time— there were the dolphins not far from the shore, leaping out of the ocean. I counted four maybe five as they put on a glorious show.

"Kids, look." I pointed at the sight about fifty yards out. They jumped up and down, clapping their hands.

Mike called out above all the noise. "Grandfather, can we swim out to the dolphins. I want to play with them."

Ralph shook his head no. "They're too far out, Michael."

All along the shore, families stood at the edge splashing in the waves, everyone excited. Memories rushed back of years doing just this. Simple pleasures of life at the Jersey shore. Were memories enough or should I move on to add a new chapter to my life? Live for the moment, Larry used to say. The key word—used to. Larry's ashes were where he wanted them. In the stone bench. Or did he? I reflected on his last days. Maybe he'd prefer frolicking with the dolphins like the free spirit he wanted to be. I'd ponder over this privately.

A masculine scent invaded my senses. Smelled good of bananas, coconut oil and sweat.

"What a great sight. And look at the children. Their faces are lit up. They're like dolphins at this age, carefree and full of spirit. Age does take a toll."

"You pay at the gate, it lifts and you move on, Ralph."

"You make it sound so easy, Claire. I'm assuming your husband died?"

"That he did and I've been digging my way out ever since. It's four years now." I glanced up at him. "How about you? Are you married, divorced, or what?"

He flashed a grin at me. "You are direct, aren't you? I like that. It's a long story. After the kids go to sleep, would you like to uh, have a drink and talk? Or how about dinner at the Island Grill first?"

Whoa. Sounds so appealing but I have to write and ...What the hell. "Sounds like fun. The kids get along so well. The dolphin show is over. Maybe it's time to pack it in before the little ones get too tired. Use the outdoor shower at O'Brien's so most of the sand stays outside and swing by in about an hour. Does that work for you, Ralph?"

"Yes. Claire, did you run a corporation? You're so commanding."

"Oh, sorry. I once was CEO of a large family and that's the only way to run it efficiently." CEO no more. Nope. Just the widow Claire.

Beach blankets were shaken with vigor, chairs and umbrellas folded and once again we trudged up only this time Ralph carried the little ice chest sparing me more bruises. Each child carried an assortment of toys. What a difference a day made. I hummed the old song and bet he knew it. Always befriend someone who knows the same songs you do.

We reached my house first. I pointed to O'Brien's. "See you soon." Patti and I showered in our enclosed shelter. I washed her blond hair and made sure no sand stuck to any sweet part of her. Then I tackled my long mane of sun streaked hair and finally wrapped the two of us in clean towels.

As I dried her hair, she said, "Granny, Mike said I'm pretty and Tony said I look like his mommy. Is that a compliment?"

"Sounds like the boys know what they're talking about because to me, you're the prettiest and nicest girl in the whole world."

"That's cause I'm your girl, right?"

15

"Right." We high fived. I always miss the first hand slap so we high fived again and laughed.

"You'll fix Ralphie Bug's kite?

"His name is Ralph Berg, dear. And yes, I'll make a tail to help the kite fly."

She threw her arms around me and we hugged. "Granny, you're the best." What a conniver and just five.

I cleaned up from a day at the beach while she played games on an ipad thingy I didn't know how to use and threw on shorts and a top. Looking in the mirror, I thought NO. Change into something attractive. Used to just grabbing any old clothes, I had to search for something kind of pretty. There at the back of my closet hung a yellow not too short sleeve cotton dress with a flared skirt. The print had a beach motif with sea shells and waves, a bit cutesy for me but it worked. Now to see if it fit. And it did to my surprise. No flab or old skin showing. At seventy, a woman has to watch out. One brush of my unruly damp hair and we were set to go.

Wait a minute, just wait a darn minute. I forgot to put on make-up. Can't go without make-up. Women of my generation bowed down and worshipped to the Goddess of disguise. Working fast from all my experience, I used the basic cream, blush and lipstick. All to go out with my granddaughter, two little boys and their grandfather. So much work. Too much, I wondered? Time would reveal. I didn't even know how long Ralphie Bug would stay.

At five thirty young boys voice's called, "We're here and hungry."

The deep masculine voice said, "That's not polite."

"Sorry."

Patti ran, opened the door and hugged Ralph. I'd have to live a long time to teach our darling girl abut men. I'd shoot for one hundred and ten and then some. "We're ready and so hungry, too. I have an SUV and car seats. Should we take my car?"

Ralph wrinkled his brow. "I guess that would do. My convertible isn't equipped for a family as yet."

"Convertible? No car seats for the boys?"

His cheeks flushed. "I uh buckled them in and placed pillows around. . ."

"Ralph, we really need to talk."

I puzzled over his carelessness as we strapped the boys into extra booster seats borrowed from the O'Brien's garage and Ralph climbed aboard my daughter's big truck-like car. I preferred a smaller vehicle or our long gone dune buggy but what the hell. Safety first. When we had kids there were no car seats or seat belts and when Larry brought me home with each bundled baby, I held them in my arms. One at a time except for the twins. How did I manage? But I did.

The mile ride was fun-filled with silly knock-knock jokes and laughter. I realized Patti and I had missed that something extra companionship brings. I pulled in to the parking lot as someone pulled out. Lots of buckles to unbuckle and reminding the kids to hold hands because this is a parking lot. Ralph listened and obeyed as if he'd never heard instructions before. A grown man and he had a lot to learn about caring for children. More questions came to me.

I took over, of course, I had to. "Okay gang, who likes grilled cheese, or hot dogs, or hamburgers. Everything comes with fries and milk." They told me what they wanted. Chocolate milk all around. I ordered grilled chicken with tomato and lettuce no dressing, very exotic palate. I turned to Ralph who seemed mystified. Snapping my fingers in front of him, I said, "Earth to Ralph, come in please."

He blinked. "Claire, I don't know how I'm going to do this."

"Do what?"

"Be a grandfather."

Chapter 3

Oh boy. "Order and we'll talk about this when the kids are sleeping."

Ralph ordered clams and paid with some kind of black credit card. All the kids behind the counter gave it the wide eyeball treatment before running it through so my educated guess told me it was a special card.

No fine dining at the Island Grill. One of my favorite spots at the shore. With the ocean so close, the beach waiting for us to have one last stroll before sunset, our new found group got sauce all over fresh clothes. All of a sudden I became Granny to three kids, mopping spills, saying "one more bite" and "finish or no ice cream" while the mysterious grandfather wannabe watched and ate his dinner. I wanted to slap him upside his head. Better judgment stopped me.

He's suffered a shock, a trauma, recently, and his peaceful life has turned upside down. *Claire, old girl, you're writing a script for a daytime drama. Calm down, eat your chicken gone cold and it will all be revealed before long.* Two hours later the children were bathed, in jammies and asleep, in my house, no baby sitters available.

I poured a glass of Chardonnay for myself. Ralph shook his head no. "Okay, it's fess up time, Ralph. You look like you need a friend, I'm here and I promise I'm not judgmental. Not after all the years I've lived."

He sat across from me in my favorite lounge chair, hands clutched so tight his knuckles were white. "My son got divorced recently; she had custody of the boys. A week later she delivered the boys to his house, said she couldn't, didn't want the responsibility and left. Desperate he called me, said he didn't know what to do." Ralph searched my face as if he might find an answer. "He left the boys with a sitter and went for a run to clear his head. Rain fell hard, he slipped. . ." A sob escaped, he turned his head. "A car ran over him. The end. The mother is gone, not to be found and I'm left to raise my grandsons. I'm a lawyer, a widower for a year, living an independent private life until just now. My son, Anthony was an only child raised by his mother since I had school, then building a practice, and never had the time to be a real dad. Now it's too late, Claire."

I sipped more wine and thought. "Ralph, it's never too late. Your son is a terrible loss but now you have a second chance. You can raise his sons the way he'd have wanted to be cared for. There is nothing like a man's touch especially with boys." I thought of Larry and all the time he spent with our children. How fortunate we were.

"I don't know how."

"Then learn. It's not rocket science, Ralph, although there are times ... and there are books. But the main thing is to listen to them, feed them well, keep them busy."

"And my work?"

"Are you working full time?"

"I don't have to. I can pick and choose cases, assign easier ones."

"The boys come first so get over yourself and make them a high priority. And just maybe some woman will fall for you and who knows?"

Night fell and waves crashed on the shore. My favorite kind of summer beach night. I lit a few lamps and found my way to the kitchen, cut up some cheese slices and opened rice sesame crackers, black olives and some pepperoni. Not bad for an impromptu repast. Carrying the tray, I found Ralph stretched out, legs crossed, eyes closed. His face relaxed for the first time since we met earlier today. What to do with a sleeping man in my living room, in my sacred home at the shore? A very attractive sleeping man. The chair back in lounge position already. All I had to do was cover him, eat the snacks, drink more wine and lock up. No big deal. Oh yes. A very big deal for me, the widow who hadn't gone out with anyone except Patti for a long time.

Washing my face, I took a good look at what lay underneath the layer of make-up applied tonight. Not bad for an old broad. Crow's feet around the eyes, lines around my mouth, no plans for lifts or Botox in my future. Face your face, old girl. You're okay. Still slim though a bit thicker in the middle. I'm not entering any contests soon. Like never. I applied eye cream guaranteed to erase wrinkles, samples from my daughter, and other face lotions for around the mouth. If I believed all this nonsense, I'd have spent a fortune. Instead I checked on the children where three slept all snug and comfy, left a night light on and glanced at Ralph to make sure he still breathed. We survived another day so I locked the doors and prayed for a good night sleep.

Chapter 4

My normal routine – rise early before Patti. This day I heard giggles and whispers coming from her room. Her sleep-over friends were good company, even more fun than who she called her little old Granny. I washed my face and recalling the attractive, sad Ralph in the living room, managed a quick fix with bronzer, blush, and a touch of lipstick.

"Hey kids, good morning. Did you sleep well, go to the bathroom, wash your hands, are you hungry?"

"Yes," they shouted.

"Shush. Your grandfather might still be asleep."

"No he isn't," a hoarse morning voice said. "And I slept well for the first time ... in a while."

"Hi grandfather." The boys waved from a distance. I wished they'd run into his arms but love must be learned and earned. It would take time. Maybe I could help in the month they'd be neighbors. Hell, I most definitely planned to. Nudging Ralph, I whispered to him. "A good start at being a loving grandparent is by opening your arms for a morning hug." And I gently pushed him into Patti's frilly bedroom where three pair of eyes watched us.

Kids respond in the sweetest way. The minute Ralph's strong arms opened, Patti jumped up and kissed his cheek. The boys were not as demonstrative, sidling over to find a space to hug their grandfather.

Chalk one up for experience. Caught up in the emotional experience, I hurried to the kitchen to give Ralph his moment.

Out came cereal boxes—no sugar—cut up strawberries and bananas, juice, milk and hard boiled eggs, peeled and ready to eat. A loaf of whole wheat bread sat next to the toaster and finally I remembered to make some coffee. *Scrambled brains with a man in my house. How foolish. Hmm, and make-up before breakfast? Who are you kidding?*

A chorus of "We want breakfast" came from the kids in a race toward the kitchen.

"Manners first. How about may we have breakfast, please?"

They grinned and repeated my words.

"Yes, you may. But first, did you wash your hands?"

The three of them inspecting each other's hands almost made me laugh. Ralph appeared to be taking mental notes.

Tony, six years old, took the lead. "We'll be right back, Miss Granny."

"My head is reeling, Claire. You make it look easy and I've got so much to learn in a short time." He poured coffee for two.

After looking at one coffee cup for four years, two appealed to me. Ralph appealed to me with his tousled hair, hazel green eyes and nice manly shape. *Claire, you are out of control.*

I pulled out bowls and spoons, napkins and glasses, almost reached for a bottle of wine and stopped myself. Major oops. "I've made a million mistakes, Ralph, so learn from me. It's no mystery and as a lawyer, you must have delved into some awful stories in your career. The boys are so willing to love you and they need you. Do you need them?"

He drank some coffee, black I noticed without sugar, and peered at me over the rim. "I've lived a solitary life since my wife died." He finished the cup and poured another, smiling as commotion from the little ones came closer. "To answer your question, Claire, yes, I do need them as much as they need me."

He lifted Patti into her booster seat, gave a helping hand to Mike and Tony, the big kid named after his dad, hopped right up.

A flurry of activity followed and after breakfast, Ralph took the lead. "Carefully take your bowls to the sink. I'll put them in. We don't want anything to break, right?"

"And spoons and napkins too, Ralphie Bug?" Patti said.

"Ralphie Bug?"

"'Cause you're like a lady bug in my favorite story. But you're a man. A granddaddy." She turned to me suddenly sad, the little drama queen. "Where's my granddaddy, Granny?"

I knew where he was. In the white stone bench in the back of the house facing the ocean. I couldn't tell my baby girl the story of how he died. Yikes.

I needed a deep breath to calm me down or a stiff drink. "Patti, he's in heaven."

"Let's get ready for the beach." Ralph to the rescue.

Forgotten for now dead granddaddy and heaven questions. Beach came first on another beautiful morning. We dressed the kids, cautioned them to wait, play on the porch until the ice chest was filled with treats, lunch, water and napkins. I selected a swimsuit, not black, more colorful than yesterday, grabbed a long rag cut from an old slip and some needles and thread to make a tail for the nice man's kite.

Ralph helped load everything into a little beach wheelie and we left for a day of sun and fun not too far from my door. He held his tattered kite with loving care knowing it would soon soar over the beach with a new tail. Admiring the way he held the kite, I pictured us. . .*Stop it. You just met him. What a great story though. Senior woman by chance meets a senior man while on vacation. My publisher waited for a new story. Well I'm living one – so write it.*

25

Chapter 5

Once we unpacked the beach wagon, I suggested Ralph dig a hole with the kids after spreading sunscreen on all of them. He agreed and I affixed the tail to his kite when his back turned away. That done I pulled out my notebook and began. "Instant Grandpa"— Working Title.

Mary Sinclair and her granddaughter Susie practiced reading from The Cat In The Hat on one of those lazy days at the beach in the town of Beach Haven at the Jersey Shore when a loud scream came from nearby. With no lifeguard in sight on this early morning, Mary, an accomplished swimmer, jumped up prepared to run. "Stay here honey and don't move. I'll see what's happening." She raced to the water's edge in time to see a child hanging from a boogie board a wave must have carried into the ocean. A tall man holding a little boy in his arms yelled for help.

"My grandson's drowning. Help. Please help me."

Mary dived in, swam fast against the powerful pull of the waves. She reached the boy, scooped him in her arms, grabbed the string of the boogie board and swam back. Laying him down, she performed CPR and using all the skills she'd learned, before too long the child began to cough up all the salty ocean water he swallowed. And then he cried, pitiful, sad and afraid. Mary's granddaughter, six year old Susie patted his back with her small hand. The tall man and the other boy were there making a circle of love and caring for a child who almost drowned.

The grandparents' eyes met. An undercurrent of gratitude, understanding of what might have been flashed between them. An unspoken bond formed.

"How can I thank you". He stammered. "Money, a reward, a car, anything your heart desires is yours for the asking. Don't be shy."

Wrapped in a towel, chilled with the early breeze, dark hair dripping wet, Mary giggled in spite of what just happened. She didn't know his name and here he stood, about six foot two, seriously offering her the moon. Mary Sinclair who lived down the road in an old decrepit beach house alone for most of the year. She did have company this summer with Susie and taught swimming lessons at the pool in town. Flustered Mary said, "Dinner would be nice." A pleasant change from mac and cheese or spaghetti and meatballs. "We dine at six." Dine. She almost cracked up. How long had it been since she'd dined, had a meal with cloth napkins, music playing, a wine list to select from. Not since her husband died and left her bereft, broke, and a daughter to raise.

Hmm. Not a bad start, I thought. Yes, it is. Work the scene, make it live.

I needed to take a walk. Maybe wonder-gramps will watch the kids while I take a breather. Then, well he can go fly a kite! I laughed to myself, sashayed over to Ralph and the kids and told him of my plan. He won points by saying "Go ahead. We're fine."

Holding my stomach in best as possible, I strode along the wet sand swinging my arms, happy inside and out for the first time since Larry passed on. *Do you see me, Love of my life? Send me a sign about your ashes. I can scatter them at low tide and you'll be one with the ocean forever, swimming with the dolphins.*

Dolphins leapt into the air to plunge back in the ocean calling to each other. *Calling to me?* Way too early for their show yet here they were, three, no, four, gracefully diving, the ocean a springboard for their antics. Yes, I decided Larry heard and sent his message. *Release me tonight and begin again.* What a quick response like special delivery or email or a text. Never could figure out how to do that particular trick as many times as Patti showed me. Yes, my five year old granddaughter knew how with her nimble fingers and clever uncluttered mind. As long as Patti knew how to hit 911 and give my address in case I fell, that's all I needed right now.

Reaching the jetty I turned and headed back. From a distance Ralph waved. Not a panic wave. Just a wave. Nice. I managed a graceful sway of my creaking hips as I grew closer. A panic wave. I ran. "What's the matter?"

"I have to go to the uh ..."

Laughing, I shooed him on, watching him run, kicking up sand in his wake. He could have taken the kids. They all probably had to go. Another lesson.

"How about a bathroom break and then pb and j sandwiches with juice?"

"Yay." Tony jumped up to display a beautiful sand castle. "Ralphie Bug helped us."

"Wonderful." He'd built a moat, turrets, castle doors and windows with close to architectural accuracy until waves threatened to knock the whole structure down.

"Grandfather said it's okay if the waves break it. We can always make a new one. C'mon, let's race to the bathroom."

Ralph, it seemed, learned fast. Day two. I had to teach him all the tricks of opening his heart and listening to his grandkids, write my story of romance between two seniors at the beach and take care of my own granddaughter who has temporarily forgotten about me. Oh, I also had to release my darling Larry from the white stone bench late tonight and what the hell would I do with it afterward. Decisions, decisions all on my little head with gray roots.

The kids raced ahead, I stumbled along, my legs too tired to go faster. Ralph, bright eyed and bushy tailed, what the hell did that mean about a human, ran over and took hold of my arm.

The day went well and once again the Berg family slept at our house. After I told Ralph I had something private to accomplish when Patti fell asleep, he asked if they could stay one more night. Then he'd be helping me the way I'd given aid and comfort to him is the expression he used. I left him drinking wine and reading a John Sandford mystery, one of my favorites, he'd found on a shelf lined with books. All my books were there, non de plume Claire Ralston, my maiden name. Pausing at the door, I recalled Larry reading aloud a passage from the same book Ralph read now. The men merged as one in my sorry state. Blinking my eyes to restore a sense of focus, I hurried to accomplish the task before me.

Chapter 6

Carefully I lifted Larry's urn and turned it around to examine any signs of damage. I pictured the shop where, on a whim one evening about six years before, Larry dragged me in to a pottery shop on the main drag and pointed at two matching ceramic jars. "When we die, our ashes can go right in there." Without asking me, his faithful loving wife, if I liked the idea he'd paid and home we went with something else for me to dust. Little did we know his heart would fail the following year.

In the moon lit night I walked down to the shore's edge, my heart splintering with every step. I pried open the lid and let his ashes drift with the wind out to the ocean. Sobbing, I walked along the empty beach front until the urn emptied. When it felt too light to contain even a feather I hurled it far as possible and watched it bob and fill with the ocean we loved so much until the urn disappeared. Then I made my way back and sat on the cold stone bench. One thought came to me. I vowed never to marry again; never to take another man's name. Never. Slow and steady I closed the short distance to the home we'd shared so many years where now another man and his grandchildren slept, my mind as empty as the urn.

Ralph met me at the slider doors. I fell into his arms and cried. Cried for my loss and what I'd just done. He led me to the living room where a glass of wine waited. I sipped the wine, stopped crying and sat quietly fresh out of thoughts for now. Single.

Ralph broke the silence. "Is this your book?" He held out my first book, *Remorse After Romance*. I sighed.

"Yes. How did you know?"

"The picture on the back. You haven't changed."

"Flattery will get you somewhere." *Flirting at a time like this.* "I've stayed with the same publisher all the years during the changes to electronic book, audio and more I don't understand. Now I feel like the Grandma Moses of Romance and Suspense." I gulped the rest of the wine and headed for my room, too emotionally drained for conversation. "Thanks and goodnight."

I staggered to my bed, dusted off my sandy feet and tried to sleep but all I could do was stifle sobs so I wouldn't wake anyone. The bedroom door creaked open. Ralph appeared and he crossed to me.

"Claire, I'm here for you. Don't be afraid." His warm body slid between the sheets to hold me tight. "If you want to tell me about whatever private business caused you to break down tonight, I'll listen. If you want to cry I'll hold you until you stop."

Too emotionally drained and too tired to say get the hell out, I closed my eyes and slept on.

In the morning we woke up before the children, still entwined in each other's arms in my sandy bed.

"Well hello stranger."

"Hello, not so stranger." I moved to get up. Ralph didn't let go. "Uh, Ralph, is this where I call the cops?"

"You make me laugh and Claire, I never want to let you go."

"We just met."

"How much time do we have in our lives? You are what, about sixty five?"

"Seventy." *I have to brush my teeth.*

"Okay. I'm seventy one with two small boys to raise. I liked you the minute we met and here we are, two days later, in bed snuggled up as if we've known each other for years. Let's really get to know each other while we're alone without anyone but the kids around."

"By really getting to know each other, do you mean sex?"

Ralph laughed so hard I hit him with a pillow. "What's so funny?"

"You. Of course sex. I want to," he whispered in my ear a few ideas he'd had in the night, "so what do you think?"

Again I hit him with a pillow and ran to the bathroom, locked the door and stepped in the shower. By the time I returned, virginally clean with just a touch of make-up, I smelled coffee fresh brewed and three youngsters gathered around the table already eating cereal. Ralph poured two mugs, a repeat of yesterday. We would remain friends, nothing more, I thought.

"I looked at a map and found a zoo, Popcorn Zoo, and playground about twenty miles north of here. Does that sound like fun?" Ralph's green eyes search mine for approval. He might have asked me first but a short trip for the day might be a nice change.

"Cool," "Awesome," yelled the kids.

"Sounds good to me, too, so it's a go. Finish breakfast, we'll pack fruit, juice and cheese sandwiches, and we can leave in about an hour – after clean-up." I sipped perfect coffee, aware of the man across from me. "And maybe hard boiled eggs." The kids were too excited making plans with Patti telling them about the zoo, one of her favorite places while we grownups exchanged a few knowing looks from our bedroom conversation.

My eyes said, "Sex? Impossible. Not after four years."

His said, "Oh yes. You'll love it and no worry about babies."

"I forgot how."

"It's like riding a bike. You never forget."

"Like riding a bike?" I pictured pedaling my old Schwinn naked. And broke the silent conversation before I ran for a pillow to hit Ralph.

"What?" Ralph made a feeble attempt to look innocent.

"I'll clean up and you help the children get ready."

I poured cold water into a pot and carefully added a dozen eggs, salt sprinkled over and I watched as the water heated. "A watched pot never boils," were Ralph's exit words called over his shoulder.

"Very funny." I packed lunch fast in the ice chest and ran to my room for a decent outfit. *Must go shopping*, I thought again. All my clothes were frayed and out of style. He sauntered past dressed in linen shorts and a shirt with tags, to my discerning eye, just removed seconds ago. *Handsome devil*. Even the children wore nicer clothes than I did. What the hell?

Ralph drove my daughter's SUV, the GPS showing us the way.

Six year old Tony spoke up from the back seat. "We have to get there real early when the animals are fed 'cause they're more frisky and we can take good pictures. And, grandfather, the light is better and you need a lens of 200 mm so you get a blurry background and the animal is clear. A bigger aperture helps. Yeah. Oh, get close to the fence to shoot. Hmm. That's all I know for now."

Ralph and I exchanged a quick glance. "Tony, where did you learn about taking pictures."

"Grandfather, my daddy taught me before he went in the rain. Way before."

Fortunately Mike and Patti were watching a movie on DVD and didn't hear. Ralph's face changed, grief written all over. I knew the expression and touched his hand. I liked the feel of him.

"Then you can help me take pictures today, Tony. You may know more about photography than I do and I have a fancy camera." A grin replaced sadness on Ralph's grandson's face.

We held tight to our precious little ones advising them to hold hands, stay close, don't talk to strangers. I had Patti's stroller for anyone who tired and it held lunch and a change of small clothes just in case.

"I've run board meetings with millions at stake and never seen one as well organized as the way you operate, Claire."

I smiled up at him, a rainbow of color flashed inside me. "What a kind thing to say considering I've been nothing more than a home engineer all my life."

"Not true, Claire. You raised a lot of children, wrote many books, and had a happy marriage from what I can tell. That's quite an accomplishment." He leaned close enough to whisper, "And it's not over. Maybe just beginning? Think it over, dear Claire. Send me a sign."

A sign. A burning bush? After a moment I nodded. We heard a lion roar. We were at the zoo. Not grand like the big one in NYC but who cared. Summer just got hotter at the Jersey Shore.

Chapter 7

One at a time we carried sleeping youngsters into my house and put them to bed. Ralph yawned, his new clothes splattered with catsup.

"Make yourself comfortable. Stay one more night since the boys are sleeping unless you want to go to O'Brien's."

He shook his head and turned toward my bedroom. "Uh, Ralph." I grabbed hold of his shirt and guided him the other way. "The guest room is down the hall. And there's another bathroom. Good night." Closing my door, I thought about locking it. Better not. What if the kids needed me. What if … ? Possibilities swirled around in my foolish head until sleep embraced this old bag of bones.

Awakened by a shift in the mattress, I wished I had a gun like the heroine in my last book, Take No Prisoners. *This is real life, Claire. Someone just crept into your bed without asking permission.* "So sorry. I have no one to turn to and I'm frightened, Claire. For the future of my son's children. All they have is me and I know nothing." He sobbed and I, a sucker for someone in need, comforted him. Rubbing his shoulders, I massaged with arthritic fingers. He calmed down, turned and embraced me. And maybe that was the moment Ralph Berg moved straight into my heart with no exit door. Once in there, always to stay.

First I noticed we fit together so well. Oh my. Stirrings began low in places almost forgotten as I felt the length of this man who smelled of citrus shampoo and Canoe cologne. I inhaled deeply and suddenly his lips touched mine in the dearest kiss. He continued the kiss. *Forget oral hygiene.* I kissed him right back with once lost fervor, parting my lips, touching tongue to tongue. I snapped back to reality.

"Ralph. No. I'm not ready for this. I may never be ready."

"Oh, Claire. You sure?"

"Not positive but I'm an old fashioned woman and this is the way it must be, so for now, let's be satisfied with getting to know each other."

He groaned. "Not even kissing?"

Ralph knew how to kiss. Why give it up? "Okay. Get out of my bed and we can kiss, but only kiss standing."

Thunder rolled across the night. Streaks of lightning flashed illuminating Ralph's handsome face and body as he struggled out of my bed. "That's a sign, Claire. Nature says we shouldn't wait."

"Close the door on your way out, my dear. This is my nature speaking and sleep well."

Thrashing around on the empty queen size bed shared only with Larry, I realized if I did get um, involved—*but never serious, remember--* with Ralph I'd need a new bed. Big purchase. *Write the new book and make enough to begin again.* Mind settled with a goal ahead, I slept.

From Patti's room, a little voice cried out, "Granny, Mikey's crying."

I stumbled from my bed and raced to her bedroom, almost colliding with Ralph.

"Mike, do you hurt somewhere?" I held him, his small back damp with perspiration, and he cried hard.

He pointed to his heart. "Hurts inside." Tony rubbed sleepy eyes and put his arms out to hold his four year old brother. Too grown-up for six, already he knew the problem. "Mike misses our dad. He's never coming back, right Grandfather?" Ralph shook his head.

I whispered to Ralph, "Embrace your grandsons. Say you're going to take good care of them until they're all grown and then they can take care of you." I gave him my fierce listen to me or else look. "Say and do right now, Ralph or no more ... us."

Nodding, a light in those remarkable green eyes, he repeated words from my script. A fast learner, my new friend. Gathering his kids in those strong arms, he assured them of a good life ahead and he beckoned Patti to join them. After sips of water, lights were out and soon peace came to my little house on the beach.

Outside we sat on the patio and listened to waves lap against the shore, monotonous enough to lull and calm our fragmented minds. We'd just begun a real romance, not fictional, and we almost went too far like going all the way. After a few days of meeting him, we were close to naked. *Claire, you are not quite a slut. Fortunately you stopped in time.*

"Claire, you're not a slut."

"What?"

"I said. . ."

"I know what you said but I just thought those words and you said them."

"We're on the same wave length."

The word *length* brought a mental picture to my mind. Like a horny teen yearning after a stud. God save me. I'm too old. Or am I?

And so Ralph Berg and I became a team after knowing each other a few days. As I always proceeded in my books, what happens next?

Chapter 8

Head spinning, I tried to focus. Are we out of control or what? A grandma and a grandpa kissing passionately so what's the big deal? Yeah like some erotic tale, uh, story. I pictured the book cover: Ralph stripped to the waist showing what's left of his muscles, gray hair sprouting here and there on his chest and me, the heroine, wrinkled boobs pushed up, flabby under arms dangling. Title: Still Hot After All Their Years. Best Seller. Movie deal.

My practical mind took over. "So you paid for O'Brien's and haven't slept there once."

Ralph rolled over and sighed. "A private moment and you bring up real estate. Where did I go right?"

"Just asking. A beach house goes for how much, six thousand a month?"

"Worth every penny, my love."

"And when my daughter returns in a few days?"

"You'll steal away in the night to O'Brien's and my arms."

"Steal away like a lusty wench to kiss standing up? I don't think so."

Moonlight spilled across his face casting shadows through the shutters. A frown creased his brow.

"Claire."

"Yes?"

"Don't laugh."

"Okay."

He breathed deep and slow. "I believe we're soul mates meant for each other."

The old song—very old song—"Heavenly Shades of Night Are Falling, it's Twilight Time" played in my head. Soul mates, meant for each other. Romance and suspense; what happens next, my writer's mind questioned.

"And," Ralph continued. I needed to sit up, belt my robe tighter and listen. He sat facing me, not bothering to tie his robe. *Men, can't live with 'em, can't leave 'em by the side of the road.* "And this. I'm a man of means, enough to take care of us. I'm in excellent health with a home on Manhattan's upper East side and a top law practice. We can date or we can cut to the chase and get married."

Married. MARRIED!?

"Oh Ralph." I held his hands wanting to punch his lights out or kiss him. "You are a practical romantic. One thing you must know right up front, I. Will. NEVER. Get. Married."

He didn't seem to pay attention ."Say yes, Claire. We'll make each other happy and be good company as we drift into old age."

The days passed in a bliss only the beach could make one feel. With the calming sound of gentle waves at low tide, the ocean's roar, my senses were on overload. And now Ralph. He did funny things like waiting 'til the kids were out of earshot and saying, "Marry me, today." Then he'd saunter back to the children before I recovered. Or one day he placed a dime store kid size friendship ring on my pillow with a card. "Be my buddy for life." With buddy crossed out and wife inserted. Sweet. I ignored his sly tricks. My mind was made up. No marriage.

"How about living in sin, Claire." He whispered in my ear at the beach.

The word sin made me tingle all over. "I don't do sin."

"What do you do, lovely lady?"

"I um, write and today I have to write. I must put something on paper this very day."

"Of course you do, my sweetheart and I must learn to be a grandfather under your tutelage. I listen to your words and repeat like an obedient student. Have you ever taught a class before?" He brushed his fingers across my cheek. The warm day grew warmer with him so close. Tenacious, this instant grandpa. He never took no for an answer. I liked a man with confidence and perseverance. And a great kisser.

I watched our little ones build sand castles at water's edge unaware of their grandparents involvement. Did we have a future together in this twilight time of our lives? *One step at a time, Claire. A future didn't have to mean marriage.*

After bestowing a standing up kiss on his cheek, I shooed Ralph away. "Now go. Have fun with the kids while I write."

As for Ralph, he turned away and adjusted the front of his swim trunks. "Sign me up for another grandfather class tonight." His laughter carried across the windswept beach, music to my ears.

Patti, Tony, and Mike blended as if they'd known each other since infancy. And Ralph became the kite maven with enthusiasts gathering around to ask questions. He had a following and they loved his tail. *Hmm.*

I made progress with my senior romance, working title: Instant Grandpa.

The newcomer introduced himself to Mary. "I'm Martin Ludlow. John would have died without your help. You saved him while I stood helpless. And all you ask for is dinner?" Tears gathered in the man's dark eyes. He held hands with another small boy.

"I'm Mary Sinclair, Mr. Ludlow. I did what comes naturally to me. I swim and learned life saving at an early age."

He shook her hand with a firm grip. No soft skin. A working man's grip. Mary liked the feel of it.

"All right then, you must dine with us tonight." He made a sweeping gesture to include Mary's granddaughter, Susie, and his grandsons.

"Where?"

"My home." He pointed to a mansion above the dunes. "I, we, John and Chris and I just moved in and you'll be our first guests."

When her jaw moved back in place from gawking, Mary smiled. "Lovely."

The children got to know each other through the day collecting shells, playing kick ball, and taking turns on the boogie boards with close supervision.

By five p.m. Mary and Susie waved bye and headed home to shower for the big night out. All day Mary had observed Martin Ludlow, lost in his role as grandfather. A successful man with two small children to care for.

I paused and thought. Is this a mirror image of my life right now with the names changed to protect the guilty? I needed a conversation with my publisher. Looking at Ralph and the kids made me pause. *Go on, Claire. This is your career, your moment to work.* Meanwhile, caught up with the story, I wrote. Just a few more words, I promised myself.

Mary dressed in a long forgotten summer gown, tied her dark shot-with-gray hair back in a clip, and Susie adorable in a sundress, trudged up the road to the mansion where a crushed shell driveway bordered with flowers put Mary's shabby little path to shame. "Awesome, Gram."

"So it is." Mary squared her shoulders. "Ring the bell, Susie.

On tiptoes, the small girl stretched to push a button. "Chimes." She jumped up and down out of her sandals. "So pretty."

A smiling young woman wearing a white apron over black pants and a black shirt opened the big carved door. "Welcome to the Ludlow's. I'm Claudia. Come in, please."

Mr. Ludlow strode toward his guests looking very snazzy to Mary's eyes. Imposing might be another word for the man.

He opened his arms and literally swept Mary off her feet with a Hollywood type of embrace.

"I'm so pleased you're here. Both of you, dear Mary and Susie. Mary, you're lovely in that dress. It's an original from France."

How did he know? Mary wondered. Purchased on a trip to Europe when her first husband was flush with success and always showing off, now the dress hung with fancy clothes hidden at the back of a small closet. What a waste.

She flushed from intimate contact with Martin Ludlow and the unexpected compliment.

"Claudia, please take the children to see the trampoline while Ms. Sinclair and I have champagne."

And suddenly they were alone with Frank Sinatra crooning through hidden speakers. The handsome stranger from the beach escorted his guest to a blue room where you had to step down to sit, many cushions on the wrap around sofa in shades of blues and purple and white distressed wood cabinets.

"Make yourself comfortable, Mary, while I pour." She sat down and an irresistible urge to curl up overcame her. A *woman who did what came naturally had no problem kicking off her sandals. She watched him pop the cork with ease and half fill two etched crystal goblets.*

Handing one to her, he sat and clinked his goblet to hers, the bell like sound only fine crystal could make brought music to her ears. His remarkable dark eyes looked into hers. "To us."

To us? We just met. I call him Mr. Ludlow and he looks at me like I'm dessert.

Speechless, Mary sipped the finest champagne she'd ever tasted. "Lovely."

"Yes, you are, Mary Sinclair."

Susie ran in, Claudia hot on her heels and two solemn boys trailed after breaking the moment.

"Grams, I just bounced on the biggest trampoline in the whole wide world. "She extended her skinny arms as wide as she could.

"Sorry, Mr. Ludlow. She escaped."

Mary opened her arms to embrace Susie. "I'm so glad you're having fun. And how about you two?" She beckoned to the small boys and pulled them on her lap. "Are you having fun with Susie?"

They looked as if fun might be a foreign word. Her heart ached for their sadness. Mary wanted to bring joy into their lives.

"Dinner is served," Claudia said.

"Come on guys, I'm so hungry," and Susie ran off to follow the maid or is she an au pair? Mary didn't know what her position encompassed in the mansion. The brothers trailed after with Mary in between holding their hands.

Tears splashed on my notebook. I love this story. My new replacement hip needed stretching and I had to walk, maybe limp along fast. I signaled Ralph. He gave a thumbs up. I walked fast 'til the story melted from my thoughts and when I dragged my sorry ass back, I collapsed on the blanket. Time for lunch. The kids ran over. "Ralphie Bug gave us lunch, Granny." "Uh huh." "Yup," Mike said and I wiped evidence of peanut butter from his chin.

"Good. And bathroom?"

"We went." They ran off to play.

"You learn fast, Ralphie Bug. A for today."

"What about last night's grade?" His arms wrapped around my waist.

Oh my. On the beach with families all around and he wanted to jump my bones..

"A+ in the kiss department, my dear. Go fly a kite before we get in trouble and maybe barred from the beach."

"Wait a minute." He breathed in then out slowly. Off to fly his kite with my old slip for a tail.

Am I the old slip now his tail? I wondered and laughed out loud. He ran, the kite lifted higher than any other fancy ones on the beach. Tall and triumphant, this man. Soon before my daughter returns, I'll see what happens.

Chapter 9

Ralph and the boys moved back to the house he'd rented for a month. Patti cried. I soothed my precious granddaughter, said she'd see them the next morning and we cuddled 'til her eyes shut tight, long lashes spread like feathers at the top of rosy cheeks. Restless, I wandered around my old beach house, sat on the back porch listening to the lap, lap of gentle waves against the shore at low tide. Ralph waved a lantern from two houses down, clicked the light on and off. *What next? Smoke signals? The fire department called by a frantic neighbor.* Using my cell phone like a grown-up, I called ready to scold.

"Hello, darling."

His deep voice struck a nerve inside and I melted. "Hi." Clever retort. "Nice outside listening to..."

"I love you." He disconnected.

And I had an inkling maybe I almost... Oh shit. I think love happens when you least expect it. How fortunate to meet a man who didn't look at my wrinkles and walk away in search of a younger woman. Humming "Some Enchanted Evening, you may see a stranger across a crowded... beach," I locked up and went to bed.

I woke up too early... Coffee. I needed a fix. I made enough for two. By the time Patti awoke I had on beach regalia. Oh for the days of bikinis gone forever and thankful daughter took me shopping before she left for vacation and bought four nifty bathing suits. I wondered if long sleeved swimsuits were available to cover flabby under arms. Patti jumped around ready to do the day with her buddies after breakfast.

Three happy faces showed up at the door. "Come in. Did you have breakfast?"

"Yup. Granpops made panny cakes 'n they were yummy." Mike laughed and rubbed his belly.

The three kids ran to Patti's room to play.

"Granpops?"

"Yup. Give old Ralphie Bug a kiss this morning."

I gave him a fast peck on the cheek and poured coffee for both of us. "Do you have a plan this morning?" We exchanged glances over the top of mugs.

"My camera is an analog so it doesn't crank out digital pictures instantly. In order to satisfy Tony, I had to send the roll of film out to be developed. It should be back today. I wondered if I could take all the kids to the main drag. I'd take Mike and Patti in a twin stroller I found at O'Brien's. Tony and I will push and watch them carefully while we get the film."

Let Patti out of my sight even for a short while? "I don't know, Ralph. She's all I have. Her mom trusted me to care for her. I'll come along."

He pulled me close. "That defeats my purpose, Claire. I want to prove I'm capable. We're walking a short distance just up the ramp and around the corner to the drug store where I paid for special delivery service. Then we'll turn around and come right back. You'll have time to write a chapter or two."

The thought of free writing time closed his case. "Promise you'll call when you get to Hoyt's Drug Store."

He kissed each finger on my right hand sending tingles to a moist place in my body. "I promise."

What the hell have I done? I thought and ran after them.

"Changed my mind, what's left of it."

Ralph turned to me, an expression of annoyance crossed his face. A thundercloud hung over him.

"What?"

"You changed your mind? You mean you didn't trust me with Patti. After all we've meant to each other."

"Ralph Berg, you listen to me. We met about a week ago. That's not enough time to trust anyone with my granddaughter. Yes, I admit to caring for you," I caught my breath, "more than I ever dreamed of but allow me to make choices and mine is to watch over her and keep her safe. You are learning to take care of small children. I've years of experience and I'm willing to share. Come on kids, let's see what goodies Mr. Hoyt has in his shop while Granpops gets the pictures."

At the back of the shop I saw a disgruntled Ralph, hand reaching for his wallet, paying, stepping aside and opening the package. His face lit up as he examined one photo after another. He hurried over, storm clouds gone.

"Check this out. Our zoo pictures and Tony took most of them." They sat at a bench with a small table he wiped clean with a napkin and spread the most beautiful close-ups of lions and tigers and oh my! Every animal they'd seen came to life so clear and focused. Ralph beamed with pride as he handed an envelope to me. "Special for you." I didn't get a chance to look until later.

"I did that?" Tony said.

"Yes you did," we all said.

"My dad taught me and I listened."

Ralph hugged him. "You did. This calls for two things."

"What?" Mike and Patti said.

"A trip to the ice cream shop to celebrate and we need an album to keep these photos in. Maybe Mr. Hoyt has a really nice one."

"Ice cream? It's nine a.m."

Ralph grinned. "Why not?"

Dear old Mr. Hoyt had kept up with the competition in town and expanded from aspirin to high end everything. Ralph found a suitable album.

Over small scoops of chocolate and vanilla ice cream no sprinkles, Ralph said he had an idea. My ears perked up. "Tony is six and he took most of the pictures, instructing me as to how when I held the camera. Remarkable, don't you think?"

"Well yes. Of course."

"I could send copies to someone I know at a gallery in SoHo with the background story. Human interest."

"Hmm. Give it a go." Opening the envelope I found a picture of me taken unaware, hair blown back by the wind, face in a three quarter shot, half smile on my face. Not bad for an old broad.

"Beautiful." Ralph kissed me. I tasted chocolate on his tongue. Sweet. I'd have to be careful of this appealing man. Very careful.

Chapter 10

Ralph herded the kids to O'Brien's to play and send pics and a story to some man he'd defended successfully, an owner of this gallery. All by the miracle of cyber space, no letter mailed and no long wait for a reply. Instant communication. I hurried ahead to the beach to save a perfect place for all of us, set up my blanket and chair, opened the worn carry all and reread yesterday's work. After changing a word here and there, my fingers flew unleashed.

Instant Grandpa-Cont'd

They dined by candlelight in a floor to ceiling windowed room, the table covered in ivory damask with napkins folded to resemble rabbits. Etched crystal bowls contained macaroni and cheese for the youngsters. Susie, ever the young lady, said Grace and dug in. John and little Chris watched her at first and followed her example.

Martin smiled. "They haven't been eating well. Susie's company is good for them. She's a born leader."

Claudia served endives with a light dressing. Mary hadn't tasted anything so delicious in years. "Thank you for inviting us, Martin. We live a simple life here at Beach Haven. Susie is with me this summer while her mom gets settled."

"And do you have an occupation, Mary?" He cut into Filet Mignon and ate a small portion.

"I teach swimming a few hours a day at the local pool." The steak called to her, so tender a butter knife could have

sliced right through. And the tiny red roasted potatoes with a touch of garlic were heavenly and asparagus with... she missed what Martin said.

"I'm so pleased you're enjoying dinner, Mary. I said we have an indoor and outdoor pool. After dinner, we'll take a tour of the house. I've seen your prowess in the ocean. Perhaps you might teach the boys to swim." He flashed a wide smile. "I wouldn't mind improving the breast stroke also."

Almost choking, Mary sipped water and wondered if Martin just made a double entendre. Palates cleansed with lemon sorbet, Claudia served chocolate mousse to the adults and the children finished a fruit dessert and each had chocolate chip cookie. Then they were excused to play.

"Martin, do you have a cook? Surely Claudia doesn't do all the chores."

"Of course, a cook. A chef, actually. Since we just moved in, there are many arrangements still at loose ends. I also have a home in Connecticut where I work and the boys will attend private school." He sighed. "So much to do, so little time. Let's take one day at a time, Mary. And now for the promised tour."

He held her hand as if she were a porcelain doll instead of the strong woman who saved his grandson's life early in the day. Caught up in a dream-like state, Mary floated along with him 'til she caught the scent of chlorinated water and broke free, sandals slapping on terrazzo tiles. Carefully Mary opened the enclosure doors and breathed in her favorite smell in the whole world.

"Oh Martin, this is. . ." She cried big dumb tears in front of a stranger.

"You are a wonder, Mary. I've never met a woman like you, so unpretentious and. . ." He kissed her. No one had kissed her in years. It felt wonderful. The maleness of him

and Mary once again blossomed into the woman she used to be only smarter.

"Martin, we just met this morning."

"I know but who cares. When I first saw you dive into the ocean, rescue John and stand there asking for dinner after being offered a car or anything you wanted, something inside me clicked and said she's the one."

"One what?

"The woman I want to marry."

Oh Claire, what are you doing? I'm talking to myself is what I'm doing. It's fiction. A story; a fairytale like once upon a time. No. It's a take-off of my life right now. Well old girl, you can't pour the ashes back in the urn. Single not double and Ralph wants double.

Ralph came running toward me the kids in tow behind him. "I have a response from Andre Galante in New York. He's very impressed with Tony's pictures and is flying here to watch him and validate what I've sent."

"Validate?"

"Of course. Why should he take my word when he can see for himself?"

"Hmm. True enough. Well this is exciting. When is he coming?"

"Now. As soon as his private jet gets take off and landing instructions."

"Now? Like in a couple of hours?"

"Yes. So let's get ready, cleaned up and whatever we have to do to make ourselves presentable."

I laughed. "You don't waste time, do you, Ralph?"

He grabbed me close and kissed the hell out of me, cave man style, I think. *Did cave men kiss?*

"This Andre person wants to see Tony and you. What in the world does he need with an old broad like me, little Patti and Mike?"

"Family, Claire. We are family. Remember the song?" He danced around me singing, "We Are Family... We're a package."

Following his lead, we headed to our respective beach houses, showered, lunched and the children played unaware of the change about to happen.

Chapter 11

A limousine pulled up to the O'Brien's and two men stepped out dressed in city clothes. I heard booming voices across the sand. "Andre, nice to see you. This is my grandson, Tony. Let's walk over to meet the rest of the family."

Nervous in my old yellow print beach dress, I sat in the living room writing as if I had well known visitors every day. "Claire, this is Andre Galante and his associate, Morrie Smith, an accomplished photographer. Claire is an author of many books and also my future bride." I greeted them, wanted to slug my idiot Ralph and delete future bride but Patti and Mike came running in and stopped short. Strangers.

"Patti and Mike, these men came all the way from New York to visit and look at Tony's zoo pictures."

"Hi," Patti said. "We went to the Popcorn Zoo and my friend Tony knows how to take the bestest pictures. Right, Mikey?"

"Right. My big brother."

Morrie said, "Tony, may I see your camera?" They walked to a corner of the living room where I heard words like focus, aperture, lighting, time of day, and all things six year old Tony talked about a few days ago on the way to the zoo.

What a difference the days made. If we hadn't gone to the zoo etc, etc. ... Chance. The way Ralph and I met. Meant to be? Maybe.

Tony led the way to the jetty where he and Morrie spent some time taking pictures, talking photography. The dolphin's appeared right on time as if they had a schedule. Known for brains and prowess maybe the leader wore a watch on her flipper. For a man who'd been all over the world, Morrie appeared to be excited with the natural beauty of the moment and Tony, an old hand, explained about the daily show and warned the man in the suit not to swim out.

We were close enough to catch bits of their conversation and like proud grandparents, *oh Claire what are you thinking*, we beamed at the bright six year old. Tony captured pictures of dolphins leaping through the air. Morrie did the same. My educated guess? They would compare them.

The limousine drove all of us to the Island Grill where we had lunch followed by another photo shoot. Later Tony drooped and I suggested he had enough. Andre nodded, said they'd get in touch and they dropped the bunch of us at my house. Ralph spoke privately to the men before they took off. Returning, a sly smile on his tanned face, I knew we had a winner.

Under the shade of my umbrella, Ralph and I watched the kids mellow out digging holes and making highways in the sand. Thinking ahead like an author, I said, "What happens next?"

"A big spread about a six year old and how he takes great photos. Plus a show at Andre's gallery next week."

"Next week?"

"Oh yes. The whole works. Publicity and we'll all go. Andre has an opening at the gallery. Cancelations happen. His feeling is before Tony is older, he wants to promote his age, the way he listened and learned and more."

"Will this do harm to him, Ralph?"

"Harm? In what way?"

"I don't know. Just a feeling. I hope Patti can come. My daughter will be here in a few days. She's peculiar about changes. God knows what she'll say about us. I mean the fact that her mother has a friend."

He hugged me. "It's not her business in the long run, Claire. She married the man she loved. You have another chance at happiness and companionship."

He hasn't met my willful, bossy, darling daughter Marissa. Hmm.

Two days later Marissa called. From Mexico City. "We're on our way back. Len got a severe attack of stomach virus and there's no point staying here. I can't trust the doctors so we'll be in New York to see Dr. Albert and if Len is better we'll drive to the shore."

"Oh, honey. I'm sorry to hear he's been sick."

"Acapulco. It happens every time."

"Hold just a minute." Hand over the phone, I whispered to Ralph about the situation.

"This might work out all right. Tell her you have an appointment in New York. You'll call when you get there. You and Patti stay at my home. We'll make a plan. First pack, lock up the house and we'll fly. It will be an adventure for all of us."

"Stand up kisses only, Ralph." He glared at me.

Fingers crossed I told a big fat lie. "Marissa, I'm meeting with my publisher in New York so I'll take Patti and call when we get there. Gotta run. Bye."

When you have money, lots of it, you charter planes, hire limousines. Not in my previous world. Patti and I packed fast, locked the house and car and waited a few minutes for Ralph and the boys. I watched the Ralph I first met so downcast and sad change to a take charge man in full command.

Comfortable in his own skin now, I pictured him in court convincing a jury to see it his way. Women must love him and yet he'd chosen me. *There's no accounting for taste, mother used to say.* Off to the private airport we went and two hours later we were in New York headed to the Upper East Side.

"My home," Ralph said pride in his deep voice when we arrived. "Wake up, sleepy heads. We're here at Grandpops house."

Rubbing their eyes, three small children looked out the window. "Where's the beach?" Patti said.

"We're in New York City right now, honey and we are going to have the bestest time. Then we'll go back to the shore."

She yawned and blinked awake. "Okay."

The spacious Boston Ivy covered red brick house had flower gardens everywhere. Lots of red, purple and pink impatiens. Not at all what I'd expected. A small grass lawn, big old trees. Beautiful and well kept.

The refrigerator contained fresh milk, cheese, eggs, fruit and vegetables. Someone had been shopping. "I called Martha. She's been my housekeeper for many years. So she cleaned up the booze bottles, cigar butts. . ."

"You devil. There's no way you live in squalor. Your home is beautiful. Let's make dinner, take the children for a walk, and get everyone to bed early."

"Grandpops," Tony called from the second floor, "all our toys are here. Awesome."

A moment of sadness crossed Ralph's fine features. "We left for the beach before I helped the boys make a full transition from their apartment to my home. I didn't consider their feelings." He shook his head. "Not fair at all."

"Honey, consider it a glitch during the tragedy. You did the best you knew how and we met. Just by chance on a crowded beach. How cool is this? We're here in New York in your home with exciting things about to happen."

"Did you call me honey?"

I ran to the kitchen, cheeks flushed with heat in an air conditioned home. *Could this be a real beginning?* "Now what's for dinner?"

Chapter 12

Andre sent a limousine the next afternoon. "Why can't we walk around like regular people?"

"There are too many blocks to cover walking with small children, Claire. This is business. Afterward we can walk, rent a stroller and check out the scene."

"Oh. And what should we wear? I don't have anything New York chic and the kids?

"The kids will wear shorts, sneaks and tees. As for you, my love," he gazed down with a look to curl my toes, "We'll stop and hmm, shop."

"Ralph, you make me feel like a kept woman. I can pay my own way what with royalties and..."

"You are a keeper...not kept. Please allow me the pleasure."

How can you argue with a simple statement? *What's the big deal if a friend wants to buy you an outfit? A very big deal, old girl. You're not engaged in anything yet more than a standing up kiss and mother said don't allow privileges.*

SoHo-- South of Houston. Greenwich Village. I hadn't been down here in years. Most book signings were in Mid-Manhattan and across the country. My eyes darted everywhere like a tourist. I scribbled names of book shop possibilities to send to my publisher as if she didn't know what went on all over the U.S. and more.

Ralph signaled the driver to pull over. We walked into a shop the equivalent of Rodeo Drive where Ralph informed the manager of my prominence as an author of many books ... and his fiancée. With Ralph's approval of my choices, we left the shop an hour later. I had two bags of accessories, two ensembles and the one I wore, a heavenly summer dress in blue looking like a Degas painting. The hairdresser styled my hair recommending a return in the fall for a cut and the make-up artist touched up what I'd done improving my beach look.

Luther, our driver kept an eye on the children under a shade tree nearby while they played with electronic devices beyond my comprehension. Soon we arrived on this impossibly gorgeous day, low humidity, blue sky, soft breeze, in front of an impressive sign, Galante Gallery. Entering, we found Tony's pictures enlarged, framed in an elaborate display. Reporters hurried over, overwhelming us with questions, photographers taking pictures of all of us. Ralph called a halt to the onslaught in the most pleasant way. His way.

"Please do not overwhelm my family. The children are young."

Andre hurried down a spiral staircase and took over inviting everyone to relax so we could enjoy the moment. "Tony Berg is six years old. He will tell you his story in a few minutes."

He shook his head, brown hair fell over one eye. I moved to Tony and brushed it back. "I'm okay, Mr. Andre. They can ask me if it's cool with Grandpops."

Ralph hugged him. Andre smiled and nodded. "Fine."

We watched while Tony listened carefully to each question with the poise of a seasoned adult. He introduced his little brother Michael and best girlfriend, Patti he met at the Jersey Shore. His story about learning to take pictures with his daddy's fancy camera brought tears to the eyes of most of the hardened reporters who had heard it all.

"Oh one thing I almost forgot. Try to shoot from the same eye level as whatever you're shooting and keep in focus. Dad said if eyes aren't in focus then uh," he tapped his head, "the brain tells you the picture is out of focus. Smart brain, huh? And one more thing, be patient, dopey."

He answered some questions and decided he'd rather eat cookies. The attention turned to Ralph. Some fool asked how it felt being the grandfather and sole care giver of two young boys.

My dear Ralph exchanged a glance with me before speaking.

"You never know what life has in store for you. A treasured son dies suddenly and leaves his children in my care. I intend to love and protect them; teach them to stand on their own two feet so they can care for me when I grow old."

Everyone laughed. I squeezed his hand. "Good job. Now what happens?"

"Tomorrow is the opening. News comes out later and on television. A crowd will come to see the prodigy. We'll see how many pictures are sold. Word will get around. A star is born. To be continued. You can write a book fictionalizing the story."

I laughed. "Maybe. Right now I'm hot on my story about two seniors who meet by chance at the Jersey Shore."

His brow furrowed. "Really? About us?"

"No, dear. Fiction. Romance."

"Hmm. Sounds like us. He kissed me on the mouth. "I'll gather the children after I talk to Andre."

I sipped a glass of white wine and decided to call Marissa. She answered moaning. "Len's improved. Now I have what he has."

"Oh honey, I'm so sorry. Take it easy. Bananas, tea, cooked rice. Patti's fine. I'll call tomorrow." I disconnected before she asked questions and hoped she didn't read the papers and watch TV. *Fat chance.* She'd be well soon and live to nag me about my friend. I have a life to live now that I'm single. A life growing more interesting every day.

Almost tripping over himself, Ralph returned. "We're going to be on two television shows this evening so the kids need to get some rest, no chocolate, healthy food."

"Uh, Ralph, what the hell do you think they eat most every day. Read my lips, big guy. Little or no sugar, fresh fruit and veggies, and so on." I wanted to smack him. I knew excitement had taken over and he'd regret doubting my judgment.

His face changed from nutsy to regular Ralph from the beach. "Of course, Claire. I got carried away." Hugging me, he kissed my cheek. "Everything I know about children I've learned from you, my favorite teacher."

Rest sounded good to me. Kick off the damn heels and unwind. TV, hmm. Been there, done that.

Chapter 13

After the two shows, we went home, put the kids to bed and holding hands we watched the interviews over and over. Tony had poise and wit for a six year old. One arm flung around Mike, he said he'd teach him to take pictures with the new Canon someone sent as a gift. Then he touched Patti's arm and said, "You too, Patti. She's my girlfriend." On the other program with Breaking News about a six year old getting his own show at the prestigious Galante gallery, the gracious hosts asked many questions. At one point Tony said, "I'm only six. What do I know. Ask my Grandfather."

I made popcorn, we roared at the coverage, kissed sitting down and finally said goodnight like horny teenagers. I wanted to snuggle up, sleep with him, make love with. . .*What's the big deal? Again I questioned why not? A virgin when I married Larry so long ago. The world has changed. Mores have changed. I made a vow not to marry again, never. Ralph ignored my protestations and guessed he'd wear me down. Guess again, Ralphie bug.* Laughing, I went to sleep.

The kids watched the family reruns of their television debut while they had breakfast. Ralph's bank of phones rang constantly. He called his office and asked the manager, Melanie, to take all calls, sort them out in order of importance and call later. We were going to Galante's for a photo shoot. Andre had a publicity stunt arranged. He expressed joy over the two TV shows and asked if we'd seen the newspapers.

Martha had placed them on the stand in the hall. Beaming, she brought several in. "Look at this." Headlines with Child Prodigy and inside on page 2, Prominent Lawyer, Ralph Berg and author Claire Ralston with their grandchildren, read the caption over a picture of them inside kissing.

"Oh for God sake. Ralph, can you sue them?"

He surveyed the picture with a smile. "Nice. I'd like a copy. Honey, don't be upset. We're newsworthy today. It will blow over and be tomorrow's old news. Enjoy the moment. Let's get the kids ready and see what the day brings. It should be fun."

In the limousine, Patti pointed to the sky. "Look, Grams. Clouds, some are fluffy white and one is gray. What does that mean?"

A prickle of foreboding crept over me. *Silly.* "There might be some rain. Maybe yes and maybe no. *Don't rain on our parade, please. Not today. Were things too good to be true? I did some yoga breathing, thought of dolphins and Larry and prayed for a kind spirit to watch over us.*

Closer to SoHo the sun came out. A clown sat in full regalia in a clown mobile. The kids shrieked with delight and ran to him or her. Luther parked, came over and showed us his badge. He was not only a chauffeur but a body guard who carried a gun. "You never know. I'll be watching every minute, Mr. Berg." He tipped his cap to me and moved away to see what the children were up to.

"Did you know about Luther?"

"Yes and I forgot to tell you. I'm sorry, Claire. I'd never leave the children without proper supervision."

"Yet you left them with me the first morning we met while you flew a kite. How come?"

Cupping her face in his hand he smiled. "Instinct. Something deep inside me stirred. Trust this woman. She will never hurt you or your boys and her daughter left her own precious child in this lovely woman's care."

"I think I love you, Ralph." I turned away and entered the gallery to see a furious young woman dressed in black, an ugly look on her face.

Ralph followed me, appearing to be on top of the world until all hell broke loose.

"I want my children. Where are they?" she screamed.

Andre raced down the stairs. "What's going on here? Who are you?"

"I'm Anthony and Michael's mother. I've come to claim what's mine."

Andre looked around the gallery. Fortunately no reporters were there, no patrons as yet. "Come to my office, now." He turned his back on the woman. She followed.

At the bottom of the staircase, Claire said, "Is she really their mother?"

"She gave birth to them. Come up and it will all be revealed. She's only here because of the publicity and what might be in it for her."

Outside a calliope played, laughter from children enjoying the clown's antics carried on the air. By contrast tension filled the plush office of the gallery. Andre sat behind a huge desk, painting on every wall and one enlargement of Tony Berg's picture of a Lion who seemed to leap out of the frame. The sticker value $6 thousand.

"Counselor, please take charge. Who is this woman?"

I sat, the woman perched on the edge of another chair. Ralph stood, confident, straight and tall.

"She's Tiffany. At least that's the name I knew her by some years back when she married my son, Anthony. She gave birth to Tony, now six and Mike, four. When Mike was two days old and Tony was two years old, she walked away from my son saying she didn't want him and never wanted his children. He never saw her again."

Tiffany's face contorted not with grief but fury and more. I perceived other motives. Greed, selfishness. To leave two babies with her husband and disappear and now she resurfaces to claim them? What kind of a woman does that, I wondered, my writers mind in overdrive. No scenario justified an action so heinous.

"I'm Tiffany Berg and I want my children now."

"No." Ralph controlled himself from what I saw although his right hand reached in his jacket pocket several times. "You see, when you screamed at Anthony he used his Smart Phone, recorded your declaration and showed it to me. As heartbroken as he was, he figured someday you'd come back if there was something in it for you. I'm their legal guardian."

She lunged toward him, long red nails ready to claw. Andre stopped her. With a voice so shrill it could cut through glass, she said, "I have a lawyer. I can sue. . ."

Ralph continued. "When one day Claire and I are married, we will adopt the boys. All they know is me and now Claire. One more thing, Tiffany." Ralph withdrew a folded paper from his right jacket pocket, the denoument moment. "This is a restraining order against you. No contact ever. Legal and binding." I watched my Ralph control his breathing and temper. "Please leave." Andre said, "I'll make sure she's escorted far from here, Counselor." He pressed a button. A minute later a burly guy entered the room. "Take her to whatever airport is her destination."

Collapsing into a chair Ralph held his head. "I knew she'd show up one day."

I rubbed his back. "She's an evil woman, my love. Well now we can enjoy every minute of this time before heading to the beach." My cell phone buzzed. I'd forgotten about Marissa. No one else called except my publisher and Ralph.

"Come downstairs immediately, Mother."

"Hello dear. You must be feeling better. I can tell because you sound kind of nasty. And honey, I don't do nasty anymore. So shape up and speak to your mom with respect."

"Mother, Patti is outside playing with two boys I saw on television and a man named Luther won't let me near unless I have proof I'm her mother."

I had put my cell on speaker, finally found the damn button, and Ralph and Andre were laughing.

"Since I was present at her birth I can vouch for you. I'll be right down." Gathering my wits and handbag, I prepared to leave the inner sanctum. "I named her Marilyn at birth. As soon as she had half a brain, she called herself Marissa. I never heard of such a name, did you?'

The men called, "Better than Tiffany."

Chapter 14

My courage wavered and I held tight to the railing in order not to fall. Daughter, a difficult kid to raise had gotten worse with age. PMS, early change of life symptoms starting at eleven? I'm a writer, what do I know. How Len ever married her was a mystery. And my Larry loved her to pieces. His baby girl. He spoiled her silly, indulged her every wish. Pierced ears at five because she cried. Too busy writing, I turned the other way too many times instead of putting my foot down to say enough. *So Claire, accept partial blame and move on.*

"Mom." Ever the honey, my son-in-law Len greeted me at the bottom of the staircase with a big hug.

"Mother, what's this all about?" Marissa shook the newspaper in front of me. "You and this man kissing —and in public! I'm embarrassed!"

I smiled at this stranger I'd given birth to thirty five years ago. She just didn't get it. Or maybe she got scared wanting me to move on and yet. . . "He's Ralph Berg, a nice grandfather I met at the beach. Mike and Tony are his grandsons. Patti likes all of them."

"But you're kissing, Mother."

"We kiss, honey." Len grinned. "They're friends."

"No, Len. This isn't acceptable. Mom said she'd never get married and I want her to move on but never change her last name. That's Dad's name, too." She sobbed as if her heart broke with the idea of loss.

Patti ran in, the boys followed after. "Mommy, why are you crying?"

"I don't like Grams uh, kissing this man."

Patti stood there, hands on little hips and looked at the news photo. "That's Ralphie Bugs. We love him, Mommy. And," she whispered loud enough for anyone in the gallery to hear, "we think someday Grams might even marry him. They like each other a whole bunch." Her pudgy arms spread wide. "Right, guys?" Mike and Tony echoed, "Right."

"Mother, is Patti telling the truth?"

Ralph bounded down the stairs in time. He shook hands with Len and introduced himself to Marissa. "You have a delightful daughter. Patti has become a good pal to my grandsons and a special friend to me."

"And my mother?"

"We are adults, Marissa and have private lives. There is no need to carry on a discussion at the gallery. This is Tony's moment, don't you agree?"

Temporarily shut up, Marissa walked with Len and after a while, I heard her exclaim, "Six years old and look at these magnificent photographs."

Red SOLD dots appeared on the frames of many pictures. Andre, thrilled with his discovery, became a talking head arranging more publicity. "We need more photographs from Tony."

Ralph shook his head. "Right now, we must go to the beach where the kids can play. I'll take the camera, of course and if he wants to shoot, I'll go with him wherever he chooses to go." He hugged his friend. "Thank you for believing in my grandson. Any commissions might go to a project for young photographers. To further interest, offer equipment. We'll think about it. Call it The Anthony Berg something or other. Foundation? Too formal. I'll be in touch."

Andre laughed. "Any commission? Tony made a bundle for all of us. My accountant will send the numbers. And you and Claire mentioned a wedding soon." *My jaw dropped.*

Yikes! "I'd like to give a gift of photographs and an album, maybe put a few copies in the gallery. This could open a whole new business for Galante."

I kissed Andre's cheek. "You are definitely a sweetie. We haven't quite decided on our status so thanks for everything. We are one with the dolphins so be prepared and we'll be in touch."

Epilogue

We herded the kids onto the private plane, Luther carrying luggage in his powerful arms. Bodyguards, private planes, luxury. What more could a woman ask for? I still said no to marriage as many times as Ralph proposed. Even when he'd suggested living in sin as a solution, an ever present twinkle in his green eyes, and I said, "I don't do sin!" he continued to have the lawyers look of 'I'm going to win this hard case.' A few hours later as the plane descended, we had a little chat while the children dozed.

With a casual air, Ralph said, "How much is your Long Term Health Care?"

"Long Term Health Care? Very expensive. I've often thought about canceling it. Why do you ask?"

"I can offer you such a deal... If we were married, my company..."

And that was the clincher. No offer of diamonds, though I knew it would be a beauty, or travel to exotic places, and that would also happen, but my Ralphie Bug nailed me with Long Term Health Care Insurance.

"So it's a go?"

"You betcha."

"Formal bathing suits? I packed my black bow tie."

"Uh, huh. I have an antique veil worn only once."

"No more just standing up kisses?"

"Nope."

YOUNG AT HEART

by
Charmaine Gordon

Dedication

Thanks to my good friend, Judy Goldstein Audevard for giving me permission to add her therapy dog Kizzy to the cast of characters in *Young at Heart*. The story is fiction. Everything about Kizzy is real. He has accomplished so much good in his life and now retires to live with Judy and Bob surrounded by a loving family.

Acknowledgements

To my publisher at Vanilla Heart, Kimberlee Williams, I give thanks for your support, shared ideas, friendship, and laughter. This is more than I ever dreamed of in our few years working together. Here's to many more.

Once Upon a Time...

"Who are all these people on the veranda and why don't they go away?"

These are not exactly words a loving wife likes to hear from her husband of twenty years. Early onset of you-know-what? Not possible since we're both in our nineties. But what the hell? I whispered in his hearing aid. "All the children have come to celebrate our big anniversary and you better behave. They want me to tell the story of how we met."

"Again?" he snorted. "Boring. Add a twist or two. Change it up. They'll never know the difference." He called for Edgar, his faithful manservant. "Bring the rowdy bunch a batch of Miss Mary's cookies."

Tall, elegant in a black suit even though we were at our winter home in St. Augustine Beach, Florida, Edgar lifted an eyebrow asking in a silent gesture if the timing worked. I nodded.

"Yay, Grumpy." The little ones climbed on his lap, knocking off the Captain's cap embroidered Grumpy. He settled them on replacement knees and patted tow heads with gnarled fingers.

Yes, he had turned grumpy over the past decade. When did he grow old? When did we grow old? I sighed and ran my fingers through his silver hair. I've loved Collin Brody from the moment I saw him.

There on a cushioned swing below sat Lindy, my grandest grandchild extraordinaire. I'd lived to see her graduate college, become a doctor and planned one day, when she married, I'd hold her baby in my arms. She waved, the bright sun catching her glow, the ocean lapping at the shore as if it too waited for The Story.

Eager tanned faces lifted, their voices raised to speak the sweetest words from those I love.

"Once Upon A Time."

Chapter 1

In a voice now gone scratchy, I began my monologue.

I've tried. God knows I've tried all my tricks to get his attention. Today might be my last chance. Known as Queen of the quip in the out-patient clinic at Helen Hayes Rehabilitation Hospital, I knew how to make people laugh. This guy, the saddest looking Irish face I'd seen since I had to pick one out of a line-up, kept to himself, never speaking to anyone except Eddy Martin, the physical therapist we shared. I wanted to share more with this stand-offish private guy. Why? I don't know. Something about him appealed to me.

"I can't divulge the nature of his problem," Eddy said when I snooped. "It's not ethical. Ask him." Eddy's kind brown eyes twinkled. "You could make the Sphinx talk." After adjusting the Nu Step machine to begin today's warm-up, Eddy left to care for someone else.

Physical Therapy was an unlikely place for dating possibilities, the slightly sanitized scent in the huge room with professionals in white uniforms everywhere. Yet I love men and they were here with me and a bunch of other women. Some of the men were too young. Yes, it's come to that. I'm in my seventies, in good shape before the surgery and determined to return to normalcy. Seventies do not go out with boys. Those days are long gone. Some of the men wore wedding rings. No way. This widow wants companionship and loving, not an affair.

Chapter 2

What luck! By chance the machine next to me was unoccupied and the Irisher tapped his way over, cane leading the way. Eddy adjusted the seat and speed, winked at me and left us alone. Well how alone can you be in a large room filled with patients, equipment and therapists? *Make the best of it, old girl. You only have ten minutes to dazzle and disarm.* I gave it my best shot with an adorable grin, dimples showing. "What're you in for?"

He paid no attention.

I pumped my legs to warm them. Undeterred by his inattention, I pressed on. "We're prisoners in a sense. Prisoners of our own bodies right now. The way I see it, we've all had an injury or surgery requiring therapy. Until we're totally healed, we're pretty much held captive by our bodies." *Still no reaction. I had to work harder. Maybe he liked the curvy red head or the tall dark haired exotic woman or...* "So I ask you again, sir, what are you in for?"

Our timers ran out at the same time and we hadn't even exchanged names, phone numbers, made a date. *How about not a word. Slow down. On the other hand, when you're a senior there's no time to waste.*

The crotchety old grump limped off Nu Step to search for Eddy. I went through my paces, shaking off the foiled attempt at reaching out. Mystery man didn't know what he'd missed.

After fifteen minutes on the step, up and down, up and down, then next on the treadmill to nowhere and last the stationary bike until my muscles screamed enough already. Through the huge windows, I watched the February weather change. Fluffy white clouds turned gray to skitter across the sky chased by a strong wind blowing from East to West over the Hudson River. Not the pretty Valentine's Day I'd hoped for and my trusty cane lay on the floor in my car.

A sudden pang of loneliness hit me. Where was my first and only husband when I needed his warm strong touch to help through this storm in my heart? But he had passed years before leaving me to take one step and another until here I stood.

Slowly I made my way through the spacious building and out the door putting on a happy face to the capable staff. I disliked saying goodbye to all who had gotten me this far. Now I had finished outpatient benefits and had to work out at home. Another step toward total rehab. Solitary and necessary.

Rain pelted against my umbrella; wind threatened to turn it inside out. I used the building as a touchstone; the roughhewn brick combined with smooth sandstone gave me comfort. As I neared my car a male voice heavy with Irish brogue, called out.

"Miss Campbell, wait up. An old man needs your help, don't you know."

The voice of Collin Brody, music to my ears, made me stop in my shaky tracks. "Old man indeed. If you're old what does that make me?"

He caught up with me and took hold of my arm. Looking down from his height of maybe six feet, he laughed. "It makes you a tasty treat, I declare."

My heart sped up just a beat or two and we walked along, me with a sense of security long missing.

He turned to me, his shaggy white hair blown back by the wind, and wonder of wonders, he smiled.

Then I recalled his rudeness. "And who might you be? I talked to you for ten minutes and not one word came back. Such bad manners I've never seen the likes of. Go away. It's too late to be friends." *When did I ever speak with an Irish brogue?*

Just then a gust of wind caught my coat and almost knocked me over. Strong arms kept me from taking a fall, my worst fear. And oh the feeling of those arms. His warmth came right through his jacket and toasted me down to my toes.

"Thanks for saving me from another hip replacement, Mr. uh." I knew his name already doing a bit of detective work, of course.

"Collin Brody. Pleased to meet up with you."

My small hand felt smaller in his large hand. "Joyce Campbell." He already knew my last name and probably had done some sleuthing of his own.

"And you saved me from another knee operation."

"Oh, I've heard tell that's a corker, worse than most. Left or right?"

"Right and so it is."

"And why didn't you speak with me inside where it's warm?"

His handsome weathered face, ruddy with the wind, turned a deeper red. "I turned me hearing aids off to concentrate. When I saw you next to me, I knew I'd need all my power to concentrate on work-out and not think about you. So here we are at last."

Blarney or truth? Hard to tell. I loved every word but I didn't know the man.

At my car, Collin searched my face as if he needed an answer.

"What, Collin?"

"Are you for real, Joyce Campbell?"

Weirdo, What kind of fool question is this? Phooey. Another one bites the dust. "I'm 98.6 and getting colder by the moment. Goodbye, Mr. Brody." Fumbling for my keys, I dropped them. Carefully he bent and retrieved them.

"Hmm. Hot lunch, is it?"

Visions of steaming chicken noodle soup and hot biscuits danced in my head. I wondered if I should accept the invitation. After all, Collin Brody was the one I'd been after. "Yes. Lunch, it is." He beckoned someone I didn't see and suddenly a limousine pulled over. A driver came around to open the back door for us.

Limousine?

"Edgar, this is Ms. Campbell. Lunch at the club." Edgar tipped his cap and closed the door.

And we were off to The River Club at the Haverstraw Marina seated by the window watching waves beat against the rocks and shore as a storm brewed. Me dressed in sweats from rehab in this fancy place I'd heard about, never been here 'til today. Waiters greeted my companion like he's royalty with the maître de escorting us to what appeared to be a choice table. Before I unfolded my cloth napkin, steaming chicken noodle soup appeared like magic, so hot we both blew on each spoon full. Collin relaxed, at home in this element of luxury.

"Do you enjoy games then?" His blue eyes twinkled with mischief and he offered me a piece of hot bread.

"Games?" I dipped the bread in my soup and bit off a small piece. "I'm too hungry to play games, Mr. Brody. Thanks for the bread. It's delicious."

"I do like a woman with an appetite."

What in the world have I gotten myself into?

"This game is called 'Getting to Know You.' I see you're worried. You thought our lunch would lead to something unpleasant, right?"

I nodded, bag clutched in hand to leave. Smoothing the worry line between my brows with a tender touch, he smiled. The gesture felt so natural my fears calmed. If he wants to play, I'll jump right in.

"Okay. I'll begin. I'm an enterprising person from away back. My family came from Ireland with a small brood of children and not too much money. If you've seen pictures of immigrants landing at Ellis Island and assimilating into America's melting pot, that was the Brody family. Skip some years of hard, good work. Lace and embroidery kept us going, we all pitched in, until Pop, God bless him, decided to get into brewing beer. Pay dirt for the Brody's. I met Maureen at a party. I spotted her across a crowded room." Collin took my hand in his. "Just the way I spotted you, Joyce. Your turn."

My turn? Collin spotted me? I took a deep breath and exhaled slowly. "You've been watching me for a while, Collin? Is that what you're saying?" He nodded and I had to laugh.

"We've wasted all this time checking each other out when we could have been, I don't know, uh going to the movies or."

"Cuddling up by the fire."

I laughed harder, almost choking on noodle soup getting too cool.

Rain beat at the windows and suddenly big hail stones pelted making staccato sounds reverberate through the glass enclosed River Club. Just as quickly, the temperature outside dropped and snow fell.

"Nature in all its fury. I'm happy to be here with you, Collin Brody. Tell me more."

He kissed my hand. "This I must reveal to you. My children, especially Karen, the youngest who has twin daughters, are possessive about me. 'Tis a pain many times. They guard me from gold-digging potential trophy wives since dear Maureen passed and they warn me to watch out for the first woman to knock on my door with Irish stew."

They don't have to worry about me. I'm not big on cooking.

We had a good laugh until I asked if the woman ever showed up.

"Indeed. In duplicate. Triplicate. I just want a companion who sings the same songs I did, someone to love again if that's at all possible, don't you know."

I do know. I patted his hand knowing deep in my heart we were meant for each other.

"And you? I've done all the talking. What do you do?"

Thinking fast, I began with the easiest explanation of what I do. "I illustrate children's books."

His smile broadened to reveal even white teeth. "Do you now? Anything I've read?"

"Yes, if you've read Super Bunny Saves the Chickens." Together we enjoyed the joke and toasted with a clink of mugs filled with hot chocolate. More and more I liked being with him. Before I had a chance to tell Collin all the bits and pieces of my life, we were interrupted.

A commotion disturbed the peaceful dining room as twin girls raced toward our table calling, "Grumpy, Grumpy." How adorable I thought until I caught sight of their mother stalking toward us. With effort Collin lifted a twin on each knee and kissed their rosy cheeks.

"Hello, Karen. What brings you to the club on this Valentine's Day?"

To me it looked as if his daughter brought the storm with her.

"This is Joyce Campbell, a friend from rehab. Joyce, meet my daughter Karen and my youngest granddaughters, Mary Ellen and Mary Jane."

Karen ignored me. "What's good for lunch, Daddy?" She pulled out a chair and called for a menu. *Her courtesy warmed my heart.*

As an illustrator I always carry a sketch pad so I have a bag of tricks especially when it comes to small children. While Collin and daughter Karen engaged in conversation, I spoke softly to the twins.

"Your grandfather has a bad boo boo on his knee. Maybe, if you sit on each side of me, he'll feel better and I have a secret in my special bag." They giggled and slid off Collin's knees to scramble where I patted. Busy unzipping my bag, I caught Collin's gruff voice asking Karen about her husband.

"Where's John today and you off gallivanting with the twins?"

"Oh Daddy, he's parking the car. We thought it would be nice to keep you company on this special day."

What do I look like, chopped liver? I thought and pulled out my sketch pad and charcoal pencil—never leave home without them. Quickly I drew simple line sketches of little Ellen and then Jane, smiling faces and long curly hair tumbling about their shoulders.

"Look, Grumpy and Mommy. See what Joyce drew." The twins hurried around to show the pictures. Collin's blue eyes lit up. Karen lowered her chin like the proverbial bull in a china shop ready to break something.

My soup had gotten as cold as the atmosphere at the table. Family affairs were touchy and none of my business. Not this wealthy family where I didn't belong and when John, Karen's husband strode in, I slipped away and called for a cab. Back at Helen Hayes Rehab Center where it all began and ended much too soon, I located my little car and drove home where I knew a bit of love rolled into one curly haired dog waited for me.

Chapter 3
Collin

"Where's Joyce? Collin Brody looked around to see the chair occupied by his charming companion a few minutes before was empty.

"Joyce who?" Daughter Karen busy ordering lunch, didn't glance at her father.

The twins said in unison, "Gone, Grumpy. The nice lady is gone."

He frowned. "When did she leave and why? We were having a good time."

Mary Jane whispered in his ear. "Grumpy, you didn't pay 'tention to her and girls feel bad when boys do stuff like that."

"Even old boys like you, Grumpy," her twin said.

Nodding, he pulled out his cell phone and called Edgar. "Did you see Mrs. Campbell leave, Edgar?"

"Indeed."

"How did she look?"

"Sad."

"Where did she go?"

"I don't have a clue."

Abruptly Collin left the table. "Business calls. Excuse me." Thundering his way out he hurried to the limousine idling at the entrance.

"Where to?"

Shoulders slumped, Collin shook his head. "I just don't know. I have no idea where Joyce Campbell lives and never asked for her phone number. Edgar, I must find her to make amends. She touched my heart. Understand, do you?"

"We'll find her. Let's do an Internet search."

The drive to Brody Enterprises in Northbrook took twenty minutes. Edgar rolled up his sleeves and began a search. Joyce Campbell's showed up in droves. Collin shook his head at each one. "She's not owner of a day care franchise, nor a CEO of this corporation, I know them, Joyce's Eatery and Saloon in Texas, not possible and so it went. Not the Joyce Campbell he looked for. Puzzled Edgar tried artists and illustrator's since his boss told him the one thing he guessed about her. Again nothing

"With your permission I can hack into the hospital records."

"Are you out of your mind? You'd be caught, the company I've built ruined and we'd go to prison." Collin's face turned red. Edgar reached for a blood pressure pill and gave it to him along with water.

"I asked permission and I agree, the idea to hack is stupid and illegal." Edgar sat back and discussed the lack of information with his boss of many years.

"Something's wrong. She's not a spy, a secret agent so all I can think of is this. Her address must be under the name of her deceased husband. No Joyce Campbell in the phone book and you don't know where she lives, do you? What town?"

Collin's head drooped. "Sad to say, I talked my bloody head off about me, me, mine, me and then came Karen and the twins, God bless 'em."

"Well then, let's move on. Since she's an illustrator of children's books she may use a different name. And, here's a thought, maybe she illustrates covers of a different type of book. Thus she may use yet another name. Sorry to say, this quest requires more expertise."

Collin poured two tumblers of Jack Daniels and handed one to Edgar. "I'm confused, my friend. Find her. I don't care what her name is. Try Campbell soup if you must. Bring her back to me. Today is Friday. Rehab isn't 'til Monday and I can't call Eddy at home, can I?" He slammed his hand down on the table so hard the tumbler tipped and splashed to the floor. "Damnation, Edgar, Eddy wouldn't have her number either." Hand shaking, Collin poured another shot and drank.

Chapter 4

"Mom, what's wrong? You seem so out of it." The daily call from daughter Amelia on her way to work. I say hello and she wonders what's wrong. Can't a mother live to be in her seventies without her children thinking what's wrong with Mom? I'm capable of taking care of myself as I burst into tears. Amelia is not only my kid but my best friend.

"Sorry to bother you with my silly problems, honey. I met this man at rehab and."

"Did that son of a bitch try any funny stuff with you? If he did, I'll kill him."

Her vehemence didn't surprise me. Ever since she was about eleven, Amelia had an attitude toward anyone she perceived as threatening to my well-being. A mini-mom at an early age.

"Oh no, nothing like that. We were at The River Club in Haverstraw having lunch when his daughter showed up and blah, blah, family interruptus so he forgot about me. I didn't fit, Amelia."

"So what did you do?"

"I left."

I listened while Amelia cursed at another driver, beeped her horn a few times as if she taught him a thing or two. "You wimped out! Mom, didn't I teach you to stand up for yourself? Gotta run. We'll talk later. Oh, what's his name. I'm going to..."

I ended the call. My daughter, the lioness protecting me- her cub. My dog Kizzy reached up from my lap to lick my face. Immediately I felt better. He has a therapeutic gift for calming me, this Bichon Frise. From the moment Mickey and

I saw him run to me at the rescue shelter, he belonged to us. The woman warned us of his shy disposition, he didn't play with other dogs and they suspected he may have been neglected, tied up. And yet one whistle from me and we were one. Mickey said, "It's Kismet." Thus the name Kizzy.

I did question my behavior the day before and decided leaving quietly was the best option for me at the odd moment.

The day planner I followed indicated exercise first, work on illustrations for yet another talking animal tale of mischief and happy learning experience. At the beginning of my illustration career I chose not to use my name. My mother, a gifted artist deceased, deserved the honor. Deciding I'd love to see her name in print, all my children's books had illustrator Rea Morgan on the bottom. My erotica book covers as a sideline, a far stretch for me, turned out to be a bonanza. I had more than a foothold in the business. And the new name Chloe Long clicked right away. A far cry from my plain old fashioned name, Joyce Campbell. Oh Mickey, my lost loved one, why did I ever fiddle around with names?

Collin doesn't know anything about me. We ran out of time. I'm not an actor, ready to take on a different persona with every role. What a dope. Every time my thoughts strayed to him, I shut down, built my inner brick wall and continued with work. Kizzy never left my side all day, his black eyes intense willing me to feel good.

At last exercise finished, I entered the small studio built to accommodate everything an artist needed right down to the perfect lighting and rags. Gotta have rags. Standing, smock on, hair up in a scrunchie, I began a new sketch with a mind emptied of all thought. A plan to render the initial drawing for the latest bestselling author's soon-to-be-released hot book titled Lady Be Bad, required no hunk with muscles, not a lot of skin revealed. Something different. The publisher didn't want same old-same old.

Snow fell, casting reflections through the skylight. Flakes large and delicate floated, melted from the heat of my room.

A face emerged through the charcoal pencil shadows I smudged with my fingers. Strong chin, broad cheeks, kind eyes wide open stared at me, the artist. I shivered, continued to draw silver shaggy hair, a glint of a hearing aid. Collin. He filled the picture and my heart. Sitting to gaze at what I'd drawn, I felt my faithful pooch jump on my lap. Once again, stroking his curly white coat brought a sense of peace.

Chapter 5
Collin

Hours later, with no success at finding Joyce, Edgar drove Collin back to his new condo at The Haverstraw Marina. "We'll find her. Monday when you go to therapy, she'll be there."

"Hmm. Keep looking, Edgar. Have a good sleep. And thank you."

Exhausted, Collin opened the door to his luxurious condo. "It's too damn lonely here. I need that woman and I'm talking to myself like the old fool I am." Undressing he replayed the events leading up to their short lunch. Getting to know her, gazing into her intelligent eyes, hot soup, twins on his lap, and then. Oh yes. Damnation. Karen in one her moods. Too young for PMS or just plain crabby? And he fell for it as always. Kowtowing to her every whim. Maureen warned him. "Don't spoil her, Collin. The other children will be jealous and she'll end up a brat. Why didn't he listen to his dear wife? And now another lovely lady may have slipped through his fingers.

Under a hot shower, he washed away his fears. Joyce Campbell would be at rehab Monday and they'd start fresh.

He couldn't concentrate. Reaching for the phone book, he almost fell out of bed. "It's Joyce's fault. She should've stayed, fought for my attention like a good woman. Damnation. The buck stops here. It truly is my fault." Reading glasses perched on his nose Collin went to Campbell and carefully checked off each name. Yes. One J. Campbell. This usually indicates a woman. He called the number and asked for Joyce only to find Joseph. He tried different spelling leaving out the p. No. Elusive like chasing a ghost, this woman who tantalized him with her good humor, sweet nature, and dignity to walk away. Oh Joyce, are you thinking of me? If you are I hope it's not with anger and disappointment. And so the night went with the concierge carrying phone books from all over the greater New York area to his door.

Chapter 6

Exhausted, smock stiff with paint, I shook my head. "What's wrong with me?" I said to the silent studio. Kizzy barked as if he too acknowledged something was off. "Every illustration looks like Collin. Even the talking rabbits." The paintings hung all over the walls. The illustration for Lady Be Bad might work. Shaggy silver hair hid his face and the woman's face couldn't be seen because she pressed against him under his chin. I ached with longing gazing at the picture. A smoky background subdued all the colors. Hmm. Different from other erotic book covers and it reeked of sex in a subtle way. I stepped back careful not to trip, aware of heat in my body like a cold furnace coming to life. *Oh Joyce, you are in deep trouble.*

Time for a bath and bed. Old bones cried out in relief when holding the rail I stepped carefully into the claw footed tub. Years of taking for granted everyday movements ended with the replacement hip. Forget walking with casc, running whenever I wanted to... *blah, blah, whine, whine.* I'm alive, in my early seventies and temporarily heartbroken. Lathering dry skin with lotion, I thought about the word temporarily and liked it a lot.

So what if the rude Irisher forgot about me for the moment. He doesn't have my phone number or address. Maybe at this very moment he's trying to locate me. Hah. In my dreams. Tired eyes closed. On the floor, after turning around three times in his bed, my pal curled up and retired for the night.

I woke up refreshed, ready to work. Coffee brewed, I looked out the window to see a winter wonderland or a pain in the back shoveling. About eight inches of snow collected on my porch and continued to fall. Pushing a broom to clear a small space outside for Kizzy who ran around in circles to be let out, he raced, came to an abrupt halt and tended to business. Four paws wiped, a can of food opened into his bowl and he wagged his tail. Happy pooch. As for me, trapped by the weather and I felt good with no distractions to disturb painting. After breakfast I examined the Lady Be Bad cover for flaws. There were none to be found.

Actually an artist can fiddle around changing a line here or there forever and possibly spoil a good take. When I started out, an experienced illustrator cautioned me to do my best, pour my heart into the drawing and quit while I was ahead. The old expression, 'If it ain't broke, don't fix it,' held true every time. Illustrators are still at the mercy of the publisher or whoever has the final say. My feeling when the cover was finished is for them to pay my bill now.

Mickey didn't leave enough insurance money for me to live a life of leisure and my experiences in the work place were basically non-existent. Craft shows where I plied my wares and drew portraits of passing strangers never paid bills. After he died I realized I had to turn my skill as an unpaid artist into a business. What a struggle to learn the how-to of computer savvy at my age. Never good at typing, even the keyboard gave me trouble but I put my nose to the grindstone and learned. I, who never handled a camera before Mickey passed on, accomplished the tricky business of taking a clean photograph of the cover and transferring it to my computer in a jpg file. Tapping the send key, off it went to the erotica big shots for approval. *Who loves my baby*? I buzzed with anticipation.

Keep super busy, I told myself. Sixteen illustrations were needed for the Bunny series plus an adorable cover. Not in the mood for adorable anything, I put some music on to soothe my savage edginess. Frank Sinatra's all-time favorites calmed me down. Bopping to "Ain't She Sweet," I tackled the first page. Super Bunny munches on a carrot. He wears pajamas, hears his cell phone tinkle with "Come Back to Me." Hmm. Funny the author chose that old song. The lyrics haunt me today, yesterday, all my days. Okay, move on to the job ahead.

Fresh canvas tacked in place, I slipped into a clean smock, paints, and brushes at the ready and went for it. I used a thin brush creating Super Bunny at breakfast, carrot in mouth, one ear way up when the cell rings. Several hours passed, Sinatra at his best, sang his heart out. When he sang "All Alone" by Irving Berlin, I cried and kept working, stalwart that I am. *Yeah, right.*

Time for lunch. Should I munch on a carrot like Super Bunny who eats only healthy food or. I reached in a drawer where way back hidden under sandwich baggies so I couldn't find it, lay a dark chocolate bar filled with caramel. Lunch! *NO, no, Joyce. Have two hard boiled eggs, a piece of toast and a cuppa tea. Decaf. Then chocolate.* Cracking the shells off the eggs, I bit into dark sensual chocolate allowing sweet caramel sauce to drip on my tongue. Yum. Licking my fingers, I rewrapped the candy bar, dessert first is one of my mottos, and had the prescribed delicious eggs and toast plus chamomile tea. Return to my friend Super Bunny and change the music. Ella Fitzgerald? 'Dream a Little Dream of Me.' Oh Yeah.

Chapter 7
Collin

"I'm up. That means I'm alive and face another day searching for Joyce." He located his contact list and called Eddy.

"Sorry to disturb you at home but I'm desperate, Eddy. I must find Joyce Campbell."

Silence in the connection. A young voice calls, "Daddy, it's for you. Some crazy man calling."

Collin shook his head. *I've lost my mind.* "This is Eddy. Who's calling?"

"Collin Brody here. Sorry to disturb you at home. I know it's against all the rules but I must find Joyce Campbell."

"Why? Is she lost, Collin?"

"Very funny, Eddy. Actually it's not so funny. She's stolen something from me and I must get it back, don't you know."

"Stolen? Joyce? Call the cops, Mr. Brody."

"Eddy, I'm a very wealthy man and I'm willing, wanting to do something for you and your family in exchange for a bit of information. Get it, my boy?"

"Oh. You mean like a new deck to replace the shambles of the old one we have?"

Hope eternal filled Collin's empty lost heart.

"Yes."

"That's against the law. I could lose my job."

"Let us negotiate in private. There is nothing under the sun that cannot be worked out."

"Hmm. Mr. Brody, I do have an idea not in any way shady. Maybe just a tad. Monday, I'll take papers out, leave them and walk away. If you happen to be early for your eight a.m., no one is around yet to disturb you."

"Monday? Man, what will I do 'til then?"

"As your therapist I highly recommend cold showers."

They shared a good laugh. "Easy for you to say, you young whippersnapper. Oh, one more thing. Is Joyce friendly with another woman who might have her phone number?"

"I'm not sure. Cora O'Brien is a possibility. And she lives in Nyack, as I recall. Her husband Larry also had therapy. So that's a lead. Joyce illustrates books. She gave me several for the kids and autographed them using a different name. Wait a minute." Eddy called his wife. "Susan, those kid's books signed by one of my clients. What's the name inside?"

Collin waited, excited for a clue, a trace leading to his love.

"Here it is. What the heck? She signed it Rea Morgan."

"Rea Morgan. Who is the publisher?"

Collin heard shuffling of pages. "Okay. It's a small publishing company called Read Away Press in Warwick, NY. Good luck, Collin. Gotta go."

"Thanks." The connection ended.

Gleeful, Collin called Edgar. "Edgar, I have a lead on my missing woman."

"Heavy snowfall happening here."

"Get Rudolph the Red Nose Reindeer if you must. We're going to Nyack."

Dressed in warm clothes and boots, Collin wasted no time. He searched for Larry O'Brien. One Lawrence O'Brien lived in Nyack. He called and introduced himself using all his charm and the rehab connection.

Things got complicated when it turned out that Larry O'Brien was with the NYPD and he asked a lot of questions. After a lengthy Q&A where Collin Brody almost asked if he needed a lawyer, Lieutenant O'Brien agreed to a meet. Cora O'Brien invited him for coffee and cookies. She won.

Snow turned to slush, the plows were out and the limousine glided toward Nyack along the scenic two lane road following the curve of the Hudson River. Collin felt the way he did before closing an important deal. The chase was on.

Chapter 8
Joyce

When daughter Amelia called, I placed a cloth over the Lady Be Bad picture and set it behind a stack. My kid had a detective sense about her. When she was little, I called her Super Baby with her X-Ray vision eyes. She ferreted information I never wanted to reveal and suddenly there it was, out in the open for her to see. Unaware of my erotica book covers, Amelia figured my income came from juvenile books. My big fat secret.

"Mom, the snow stopped, streets are clear and Lindy's asking to play with you. Okay if I bring her over? I can drag the sled and..."

I'm just a grandmom who can't say no. "Of course. Her smock and easel are waiting. Kizzy can't wait. We'll paint and maybe bake cookies."

Fortunately we live in the same neighborhood just far enough not to see into our own yards. Pearl River is a friendly town where neighbors lend a hand if necessary. Peaceful on my street where older folks reside. Amelia, Bud and little Melinda live a block away where there are lots of youngsters.

Saturday would pass quickly with my granddaughter and when she left, I had work to do. *And Sunday? Will I cry and wonder if Collin is looking for me or maybe I can call him. Why not?*

I called information and asked for Collin Brody at the Marina in Haverstraw. Private number. Not listed. Of course his number wouldn't be listed, a big shot with a limousine. You idiot! In a feeble attempt to be resourceful, I wondered if Eddy had his number. Of course not. Two strikes, Joyce. Resolving to make a plan if he didn't find me, I decided to camp out at rehab Monday, just near the front doors and bump into him. Just like a teeny bopper. Ridiculous.

The front door opened with a swoosh of cold air. Feet stamped snow off boots and voices of my loved ones filtered all the way to my studio at the back of the old Cape Cod style house purchased long ago. "Grandmommy, I'm here." Lindy flung her cold cheek against mine planting kisses and warming my insides. Kizzy came running and danced in a circle on his hind legs to see his little girlfriend. Lindy gave him a biscuit.

Amelia, eagle eyes searched my face for signs of sadness, finding none she stayed a while. "What are you working on, Mom?"

"Super Bunny and the Lost Cell Phone. He's an amusing character. I enjoy the author's story telling. The illustrations come easier when the story is clear."

"Let's take a look."

Lindy led the way to the studio and giggled when she saw the finished pictures. "He's so cute, Gram. I tell all my pals at pre-school you're the artist. When I grow up, I want to be just like you."

I tied her smock in place and shrugged my shoulders to show Amelia not to worry. If I were a plumber, she'd say the same thing.

"Why did you use grandma's name as illustrator instead of yours? I never understood the reasoning."

Steam rose from homemade hot cocoa as I poured some in two big mugs and one small marked Lindy. Delicious on a cold winter afternoon. We sat, sipped and I explained.

"Mom had a gift. You've seen several of her paintings at MOMA. Dying at an early age ended the talent and she had so much to give." My daughter held my hand, tears in her big brown eyes so like Mom. We drank from the big mugs and Lindy took hers to the easel, sipped leaving a chocolate mustache on her upper lip. "When I got my first job, the publisher asked about my name. Did I choose a pen name or my own? I heard my mother's voice call out, "Choose me." And I told her Rea Morgan is the name I wanted for illustrator. Now Mom has daily recognition in thousands of homes and book stores all over."

"But Mom, how about you? No one knows you're the artist."

"At the time, I needed to do what I did, honey. It's no big deal. I still get paid." *If Collin knew, he'd track me down and be at my door saying sorry.*

Gathering the mugs, wiping Lindy's mouth, Amelia headed for the kitchen and came to kiss us good bye. "I'll be back in a few." She locked the front door and we were alone. At last. Let the fun begin.

The cell phone sang out. "Chloe Long, please."

OMG, it's the call about the Lady Be Bad cover. "Yes, it's me. Uh, her speaking. Who is this?" *I sound like a nitwit.*

"Best of the West Publishing, Ms. Williams is on the line."

Kizzy jumped on my lamp to soothe me. Lindy dabbed more paint on the paper and finger painted to her heart's content.

"Chloe Long, your latest cover is, hold the line a moment," she spoke to someone else, "I said black coffee, the dark and dangerous type, and back to me, "your cover is hot, perfect. I like your style and plan to use your talent for a long time. No more freelance, Ms. Long. Got it? I'll send a contract to you right away." The call ended.

Stunned, I sat there tears streaming, Kizzy licking as fast as they fell. "Gram, did somebody hurt you?"

"No, honey." I sniffled. "I'm happy. Sometimes people cry when they're happy."

"Oh, Gram. You're silly. Let's bake some cookies, 'kay?"

"'kay." We washed our hands and I watched Lindy race Kizzy to the kitchen. *My big break at last and I had no one to share the amazing news. Real money to fill my piggy bank. I wish I could skip but my skipping days ended with the new hip.* I pictured telling my daughter. "I just signed a contract with a big Erotica publishing company. Isn't that terrific? Spread the word. Tell all your friends on Facebook and Twitter." Her pretty face would turn red and stern. Thin lipped, she'd say Mother using several diphthongs. Secrets. Like many people, I have a secret.

More chocolate bits were consumed before they made it to the batter. I had to call a halt. "Lindy, you and I are out of control. Let's settle down and stir in the bits. You can spoon cookies on the cookie sheet and lick the bowl but not 'til most of the cookies are placed nice and neat."

Mischief in her big blue eyes alarmed me. I had to watch this munchkin every minute. Scooping too much batter in a tablespoon, she bit off a chunk, dropped some on the floor where Kizzy's tongue made it disappear and as an afterthought, Lindy dropped a shapeless small piece on the cookie sheet. Then she smacked it in the middle with her fist to spread and gave me an angelic smile. My little doll. I helped move the baking process along, every perilous step thinking next time she'll be older and more adept. Hopefully so will I.

Cookies, milk, a cuddle up while I read to my little four year old. With Kizzy on her lap, Lindy concentrated on words and read with me, sometimes saying a word before I did. My dog has the ability to bring out the best in people. *I wondered if Collin had Kizzy on his lap right now, would that lead him to me? Silly old fool. Whatever will be, will be. Yes, but I believe in making things happen. Joyce Campbell, a voice inside me said. You've made a difficult trail to follow with all the names. Keep it simple, stupid!*

The turn of a key in the front door changed the quiet in my small house. Shrieks of Mommy's here and dog barking a greeting, cold air swooshing in, daughter entered with a flourish. Sniffing the aroma of cookies, she kicked off her boots, dropped her coat, picked up Lindy and ran to the kitchen calling, "Hi, Mom," over her shoulder.

Soon, I thought, *very soon this house will be restored to peace and quiet.*

Chapter 9
Collin

Edgar drove down Broadway where large old homes from another era were built. Helping Collin up the wide gray painted steps, Edgar waited until the wide oak door opened. Turning to leave and wait in the limousine, a deep voice called out, "Please come in. Welcome to the O'Brien's."

"I'm Collin Brody and this is Edgar."

"Yes. I've vetted you. Larry O'Brien here." They shook hands. Their host gathered their coats and led them into a comfortable worn room obviously abused by kids of all sizes. "My wife Cora is eager to meet you and we both want to learn more about your quest and what we can legally do to help." A tall, powerfully built man about forty plus, Collin guessed, his gray hair trimmed short, he had a military bearing and a nice smile.

"We have Helen Hayes Rehab in common, I understand. And Cora, she'll be in soon, was friends with Joyce Campbell. You and Joyce met, are attracted to each other, had lunch at The River Club where she left and you don't know how to find her."

"Larry, you cut to the chase. No nonsense. Joyce is an illustrator of children's books under a different name. Rea Morgan is her mother's name. Also Joyce left before we exchanged phone numbers and addresses."

Larry leaned forward invading Collin's space. "Didn't she want you to know her private information?"

Sitting tall and straight, Collin stared at him. "This is the truth. We were engaged in getting to know you conversation over lunch when my daughter burst the bubble by intruding and I, the fool, allowed her to take over the conversation. Joyce left. I didn't even notice. Larry, I must find her to apologize. This may sound foolish to you, a policeman. But we're not young and there's no time to waste."

Cora had taken a chair and listened to every word. "Let's have a beverage and sandwiches. Afterward, Larry and I will help you, won't we honey?"

The charming Cora took over. Collin and Edgar exchanged looks watching the interplay between husband and wife. Petite with red wavy long hair in a ponytail, Cora appeared to be a teenager. Her tough Irish nature showed through as she organized everyone in the spacious old fashioned kitchen and assigned tasks. Indifferent to Collin Brody's status as an extremely wealthy man, she had him slicing ham after making sure all hands were washed. Edgar sliced tomatoes and red onions while Larry toasted rolls. Sandwiches were assembled and they entered the dining room.

"Beer, wine, tea?" Larry grinned. "I sound like an airline steward. What's your pleasure?"

"Bring it on, Larry. Let's get started before the kids come barreling in. Eat, drink and talk."

Cora, a woman of action, Collin thought. Wonderful. He sipped red wine and enjoyed the best lunch in a long time.

"Who's the publisher of the children's books?" Larry took a long pull from his beer bottle. His notepad lay on the table.

Cora opened the book she had. "Read Away Press in Warwick, NY." Larry wrote it down.

"And her deceased husband's name?"

Collin sighed. "I don't know. We never got that far in our conversation."

"Okay. I'll try to reach the publisher right now. It's Saturday. Who knows if anyone's there."

He called information and got the number. Collin tensed. No answer. "I'll call Janis. He owes me big time. He can get through as police emergency."

"Wait a minute. How about looking up Joyce's mother's obituary. Children are always listed as next of kin." Larry jumped up, grabbed Cora and swung her around.

"Brilliant, girl. Of course." Digging back in the obit archives, he found Rea Morgan. Listed was a daughter Joyce married to Michael Campelli, and one granddaughter Amelia.

"Campelli? Her husband must have Americanized his last name to Campbell for business reasons." Collin wondered.

"Odd in this century when even film stars keep their real names." Larry made a note. "You never know. Now look in the area phone books for Michael Campelli."

Cora did and yelled "Bingo. Collin, I do believe we might have found your lady in Pearl River about twenty minutes from here."

Collin stood up suddenly, pounded his fists against the table and fell to the floor hitting his head against a sharp corner of the chair on the way down

Chapter 10
Collin

Words swirled around not quite clear. *Why don't they speak clearly? Didn't anyone teach them proper English?* Edgar. He tried to call for his best friend. A firm touch to his hand, the squeeze of a blood pressure cuff as it pumped, pump, pump. A crisp voice cut through the fog. "BP still low. Temp normal. Is Dr. Barry here yet?"

"Mr. Brody, have you been bungee jumping again?"

Collin opened his eyes to find internist, Dr. Marcus Barry smiling down at him. His mind cleared. "One minute I'm in Nyack having lunch with friends and the next, I'm in a hospital. What happened?"

"Evidently your friends told you something so extraordinary, your blood pressure spiked and you fainted. They called 911and here we are at Nyack Hospital. Did you take your blood pressure meds today? They're meant to lower your pressure, not to make it elevate."

Collin frowned. "I can't recall. Maybe I took three. I'm too preoccupied with a lady and trying to find my lost love, don't you know."

"Mr. Brody, we've discussed this before. You have high blood pressure which can lead to serious complications like stroke and heart disease. That's why I prescribe the meds. So if you want to find this woman and live a long life, you must take care of yourself. You'll have to stay here for a couple of days while you stabilize. To make matters worse, you may have a concussion from hitting your head. The wound required stitches."

"Wound? What else happened? You make it sound like I was in a fight at a bar."

"It's not funny, Mr. Brody. I used a sewing machine to patch you up. What a mess." The doctor allowed a grin to lighten the mood. "I stitched it and you're scheduled for a CT scan soon. Should I call your family?"

"Damnation, Doc. No. The only one I want is her. Joyce Campbell. We're hot on the trail now. She might live in Pearl River. Let my friend Edgar come in and have someone bring a comfortable cot for him. He's good company and knows when to cool me down."

"Hmm. Perhaps a therapy dog might help."

"Therapy dog?"

"Yes. With your permission, I'll call a canine trainer in Rockland County and ask if she can recommend one. I've seen them work wonders with high blood pressure patients. Meanwhile sir, take it easy, follow orders so you can go home. Edgar is outside. Nice man. Does he always wear black?"

"He does?"

"I'll be back later and tomorrow." He squeezed Collin's foot and left.

Just outside the private room Edgar sat tall and straight. When Dr. Barry came out, Edgar stood. "Your friend, Mr. Brody needs to calm down, take his meds and rest for a couple of days. He wants you to stay in the room with him. I can't stress enough the importance of him relaxing. He seems obsessed with this woman."

"He is."

"Then you must find her and bring her here to help him recover. Please."

"That I will."

Lieutenant Lawrence O'Brien strode down the hall. "How is he?"

"High blood pressure. He didn't take his meds today."

"That's dangerous. Edgar, I'm on duty this afternoon until late. I'm pulling in some markers to find Joyce Campbell or Campelli. You're staying here?"

"Indeed. Right in the room."

"Here's my card with our home number and all the other numbers. Call Cora if you need a decent meal. Give me your number." Edgar handed him his card. "He'll be all right. I have a feeling we'll find his Joyce by tomorrow."

Chapter 11
Joyce

Working steadily after Lindy and Amelia left, I almost missed the musical call on my cell. Eternal hope sprung to my chest. Breathless, I whispered, "Hello."

"Hi, Joyce, it's Pat from Canine Trainers. Are you napping?"

Deflated I said, "No. I am working. What's happening, Pat? You're calling because you need Kizzy, my wonder pooch."

"Right. There's a patient at Nyack Hospital who needs TLC from a special therapy dog just like your one and only. What does his calendar look like either later today or tomorrow?"

"Wait a sec." Thumbing through my appointment book, I sighed. "I'm booked but maybe my daughter can bring him over to spend a half hour with the new patient. I'll call you right back."

"Thanks, Joyce."

Amelia, always ready to lend a hand, said she'd spare an hour since Bud, her dear husband, was home playing with Lindy and a pot roast cooked in the Crock Pot.

Pat, thrilled with the quick response, gave a few instructions. "Tell Amelia she won't be allowed in the private room. A nurse accustomed to working with therapy dogs will take Kizzy in to do his job. Amelia can wait in the cafeteria or in the patient waiting room and someone will bring Kizzy to her. Make sure he's wearing his I.D. tag and Amelia has her corresponding number. Are we clear?"

I almost said, "Roger that," and restrained myself. Pat was right. Anyone might walk off with a therapy dog. The training the dogs go through is arduous and takes time until they are certified. Valuable, these special animals. Now I'd almost be able to finish the latest Super Bunny without disturbance.

Amelia came and went, printed instructions in hand, Kizzy in his carrier case in her other hand and my little old house settled in to creak and groan like me. Instead of going back to painting as planned, I decided to listen to music, this time oldies. When "Where or When" played instead of crying I decided to celebrate my contract with Best of the West Publishing by opening a split of champagne. "Here's to my career as an erotica cover artist." I sipped. "And here's to um, Collin Brody in hopes of his appreciating and loving me the way it should be." Another sip. I drank and toasted to Mickey, Mom, Kizzy, all my loved ones and soon the small bottle for two emptied just like me, the house. I never could drink. Heavy eyelids grew heavy and I slept.

Chapter 12
Collin

Nurse Randall entered the quiet room where the silver haired man lay still, a book on his chest, eyes half closed. "You have a special guest, sir." She set the carrying case on the floor next to the hospital bed and lifted Kizzy, talking to him. "This man needs your help." She placed the white curly haired dog on the bed. He sniffed his way up to the patient and nuzzled under his chin.

The warmth Collin felt moved him to tears. Kizzy licked them away doing his job, taking care. "Well, hello. And who might you be?" Collin peered at the collar. "Hmm. Kizzy." He received a few licks from the eager pink tongue in response to his name. "Edgar, we have a visitor. This must be the therapy dog Dr. Barry spoke of. What breed?"

Edgar glanced up from a book. "Bichon Frise, a very companionable small lap dog."

"You know everything."

"I do."

Snuggling, Kizzy at his best, Collin felt tension soften and confidence restore. Fear he'd never find Joyce drifted away as he stroked the warm curly body over and over. His lined face lay against the dog; he knew his blood pressure stabilized with each breath. Kizzy nudged the book sending a message for Collin to read. In an Irish brogue, Collin spoke words softly. "Wherefore art thou, dearest Joyce," his take on Romeo and Juliet with a happy ending. All would be well with so many reaching out to help in his quest to return to good health and love to his life. Bereft after a half hour when his furry friend had to leave, he asked about the owner. "I want to thank whoever cares for Kizzy and make a donation to the organization that arranged this visit. Also when can Kizzy come back?"

Tight lipped Ms. Randall was adamant when Collin attempted to charm her. "Sorry, Mr. Brody. The information is private. Your therapy dog is scheduled to return tomorrow morning. That's the good news. Dinner will be up shortly. No salt, butter, fat, cheese, skim milk. Your typical high blood pressure dinner."

"Yummy," Edgar said. "I'll call Cora."

"You will share."

"Fat chance."

Chapter 13
Joyce

"Mom, wake up." Kizzy danced around me as I blinked awake. "Champagne? A celebration for what? Must be something good for this and to drink alone? Really, Mom."

"A new contract and no one around. Not even my pet. How did it go?"

"The word is wonderful. The best therapy dog in town. You can be very proud. He's invited back tomorrow morning. Can you take him or I can. It's President's Day so I'm off."

"Good. And thanks. You better get home. I'll feed us and get to bed early. I'm almost finished with the latest Super Bunny. Tomorrow's the deadline."

Amelia left and I rewarded my best therapy dog in town with moist food and biscuits. Bundling up, careful not to slip and break anything, we walked around the block. The night sky sparkled with stars after the storm. I inhaled the dry cold air and exhaled loving the puffs of steam from my mouth. Kizzy checked out his usual favorite trees, met with a neighbor's black Lab off leash, strictly forbidden, and sniffed as if they hadn't done the same thing a million times. Suburbia. What fun. Then home again, home again to dream my impossible dream.

Over hot chocolate the next morning, after Amelia left with Kizzy, I re-evaluated the situation. Booting up my computer, I Googled Collin Brody. A gazillion hits. He's a super wealthy self-made man. I made a chart on Microsoft Word.

Pros/Cons

He's a billionaire. I'm a woman just getting along on Social Security and illustrating book covers.

I live in a tiny old Cape Cod house, do my own housework, no luxuries, and drive an old VW. He has a driver and a limousine.

My daughter is a loving person. He has one daughter I've met who hates me.

We. Don't. Fit. Case closed.

Hysteria took over with a fit of laughter. Forget Collin Brody and move on. *But I can't. Yes, I can.* Be grateful for all the good things in my life, nitwit. *I want more. I want him.* Multiple personality time, Joyce. *Kizzy, come back and make me feel better. Who is this stranger taking up your time? Surely he or she can't need you more than I do.*

Super Bunny took on a different look as I painted the next morning. Older, more mature with fur turned gray. What am I doing? Just because the publisher said the author signed off on the successful series didn't mean he should age. Yet here he was. Super Geezer. I laughed and almost fell, choking on dregs of lukewarm cocoa. Adding scarred knees and a cane in the corner of the picture did me in. With no one to share the moment, laughter turned to sobs. I sat and thought. What if's came to mind. What if he tried to find my name in the phone book? He didn't know where I lived, what town, and no one to ask since Helen Hayes Rehab was closed until uh, oh no, 'til Tuesday because of President's Day Monday. And today is Sunday.

Where oh where did I keep the elusive phone book? Under the phone in my bedroom I spied the bright yellow book and looked myself up only to find no Joyce Campbell listed. Dummy. I never added my name after Mickey died. Michael Campbell wasn't listed. And then I remembered. He kept the family name because our house was listed under

Campelli. Michael Campelli. His father's name. Oh Mickey, what a tangled web. We shoulda, coulda and never got around to changing the name. His dad put a heavy foot on Mickey's heart and refused to let him change the decent name they brought from the old country to America, in steerage he said to make Mickey cry. Actually they were comfortably well off and ready to start a business upon arriving at Ellis Island. Mickey was the son who had no business sense, just the dearest man in the world who loved and provided for our little family. I had no business savvy either and learned late, just enough to get by.

A famous quote from Shakespeare came to me. "What's in a name? A rose by any other name would smell as sweet." True. I resumed painting. Instead of a cabbage patch for my Geezer Bunny to stand in, I drew roses. Climbing pink roses, yellow rose bushes, delicate Peace roses with a touch of blush and in his extended paw he held a red, red, single rose tied with a white satin ribbon. Oh my.

Chapter 14
Collin

"Edgar, I need you, right now."

Edgar met his best friend's eyes with close scrutiny. "You didn't say the magic word."

"Damnation, Edgar, do you want my blood pressure to spike again?"

"Hmm. So now you're playing the health card, is it?

Together they shared a laugh. Then one of the wealthiest men in the world scowled, his Irish face lost the smile.

Edgar moved his chair closer to the hospital bed. "You're getting impatient. You want information leading directly to Joyce Campbell and you want it now. And you want out of the hospital back to your own space where you may brood, toss back a glass or two, dine on what you choose without anyone looking over your shoulder. Does that sum up the mood you're in?"

"Ah, 'tis so. You know me so well. But, me boyo, there's one little item you've omitted."

Edgar shook his head. "I can't wager a guess."

"I want the pooch." He grinned. "Before long Kizzy will be mine."

It was Edgar's turn to frown. "The four legged creature belongs to someone who loves him. Another Bichon Frise can be available if you really want a dog."

The nurse bustled in. "Your blood pressure is up, Mr. Brody.

"How do you know? You haven't been in yet."

"The monitor tells all, Mr. Brody. No secrets. I have meds for you and breakfast. Later your therapy dog is coming to visit. Isn't that nice?" She took his temp, wrote numbers on a chart and left the door open.

Edgar closed it.

"You have something else on your mind."

His mouth set in a thin line. "Take notes." Edgar opened his I Pad and tapped. "Call Larry O'Brien. What progress has he made regarding the Campelli name? Ask him to visit here ASAP and smuggle some goodies from Cora's kitchen." Distracted by a sound outside Collin glanced out the window. He thought he heard rain falling. Buckets of rain, a solid sheet of rain or was it tears from the loss of a woman he knew would fit perfectly side by side 'til the end. Shoulders slumped in despair as he pondered his place in a world without Joyce.

Moving the chair away from close proximity to his friend and employer, Edgar called the O'Brien's number.

"Lieutenant, sir. This is Edgar calling from Nyack Hospital. I fear Mr. Brody is going into a major slump. Have you any good news?"

"Top of the mornin', Edgar. No need to sir me. Call me Larry." Papers rustled. "We've located information about the Campelli family. I'm getting closer to information about a son, Michael Campelli, now deceased. His father built a small house somewhere in the town of Pearl River, New York and deeded it to him. More forthcoming news should break the case and solve the whereabouts of Joyce Campbell. It's Sunday. The courthouse is closed. Edgar, what can I do for him this morning before I'm on late duty?"

"Himself has requested a treat from Cora's kitchen. Between us, Collin Brody is known for his generosity. Kindness means a lot for my gentleman."

A hearty laugh came through causing Edgar to hold his ear. "Nicely put and a crock if I've ever heard one. Cora will be pleased to wrap up a delicacy or two. See you soon."

With a question in his eyes, Collin Brody received an answer from a brisk nod.

One poached egg next to one slice of toasted wheat bread, two crisp pieces of turkey bacon and margarine wrapped in a miniscule packet of gold foil to resemble butter lay on a dish on the tray. Collin sniffed at breakfast like a dog not sure if anything this good smelling might also be healthy for him. Edgar took one glance and asked if there was another breakfast available similar to the private patient.

Sally, the young nurse said, "We knew you'd enjoy a breakfast like Mr. Brody's so we got permission to order two. Enjoy." She giggled on the way out. "I'll bring your tray right in."

Savoring every bite, wishing for more toast to mop the plate, Collin finished. He showered and shaved in preparation for a visit from what he thought of as his dog. A possessive man, his needs had grown stronger with age. Pacing the floor, he checked his watch. "Kizzy's late."

"He doesn't drive. Just like you, he has a chauffeur."

"Are you implying I'm a dog, Edgar?"

"When you bark, there is a remarkable resemblance."

Collin stormed to the bed, face changing color when a knock at the door interrupted his temper.

The experienced therapy dog nurse, Ms. Randall, entered with the important visitor on a lead. She unclipped the dog and spoke softly to him. "This man needs your help." And the smart white dog with black eyes jumped right up on the hospital bed to visit. Sensing agitation in the man, a pink tongue licked Collin's big fist until it relaxed and opened. First Collin's large hand stroked the white curly hair over and over... the little dog nestled under the big chin to feel his now familiar friend's breathing slowed. A few quick nudges with a wet nose and Collin laughed.

"So you want me to read a story, do you?" Edgar handed the book of Shakespeare's plays to his longtime employer. "A story with a court jester to make you laugh or..."

Voices at the door interrupted the Irisher's conversation with his therapist.

"He's busy right now and cannot be disturbed."

"I'm Lieutenant Lawrence O'Brien of NYPD with business for Mr. Brody."

"Before the Lieutenant huffs and puffs and blows the door down, Nurse Randall, please let him in. He's a friend of mine."

"Not a friend of ours," muttered Edgar, mimicking a line from some mob movie, maybe Goodfellas.

"I heard that." O'Brien settled in a guest chair near the window. "I see you have company."

"My therapist. Kizzy meet Larry. He's informal. Before he arrived I was almost ballistic but a few minutes with my curly haired pal and I settled down. Almost mild mannered, don't you know." A milk bone treat appeared from under the white hospital sheets for his therapy dog was greeted with joyous tail wagging, standing on hind legs to settle and crunch. "Speak to me, Larry."

"The name Campelli Construction was once important. The youngest son, Michael, chose not to carry on in the business. His brothers have done very well combining their skills with other companies to form one large corporation. Michael was thought to be um, different from the sturdy family members because he liked to decorate and design. His father bought acreage and built a small house somewhere in the Pearl River area after Michael surprised everyone when he married and presented them with a grandchild. There's more to be uncovered but I'm sure we're on the right track, Collin."

Again the pink tongue licked his clenched fist. *I must wait and calm down. 'Tis not my style, he thought.* Eyeing the wrapped package the Lieutenant carried in one hand, Collin lifted his bushy white eyebrows. "You've smuggled contraband into the hospital. Shall we report him to the front desk, Edgar?"

"Open Sesame. Treasures await."

Larry handed the package to Collin. "Does he always talk like that?"

"Like what?"

The heavenly aroma of chocolate released once Edgar untied the colorful red satin ribbon. "Don't go telling me it's fudge now.

The rangy lieutenant stood, smiled and straightened his uniform. "I won't then. This is what my fair Cora calls a substitute healthy version of fudge. Her secret recipe guaranteed to please the palate. Also a tasty treat."

The last words caused the older man to wince. He remembered calling Joyce a tasty treat when they met outside of rehab in the blustery wind. Just two days ago. Valentine's Day. *Smooth talker*, he thought. *First I scared her and then daughter Karen showed up to ignore her. That's no way to act toward a special lady. He'd make it up once they found each other.* He bit into a square of ersatz fudge and smacked his lips. "Delicious. Cora deserves a reward for her kindness and ingenuity.

Larry shook his head. "No sir. She loved making this for you and Edgar, of course. No reward. No statue erected in downtown Nyack to honor my bride. By tomorrow, if all goes well you should reunite with your lady." Collin felt an emptiness as he watched the young Lieutenant leave with all his vibrant energy. Aging was only for the brave.

Soon, he said. "Do you believe?"

"That I do. Pass the fudge. Your four legged friend is poking his wet nose in the box. I fear for the content's safety."

Another milk bone mysteriously appeared in Collin's hand. Kizzy performed a happy dance and settled down. "Too many distractions for serious work today, my furry friend. We won't report our time off." He glanced up to meet his companion's stern gaze. "You fear I'm too attached to him and you're right. Spot on. That can be fixed, Edgar."

"Money can't buy everything."

The therapy nurse knocked and entered. "Time's up this morning, Mr. Brody. Kizzy has an appointment this afternoon at West Point. He works with special needs children of deployed service personnel. Would you like to book one more session before you leave? I checked and you may be discharged tomorrow." She reached to attach the lead. Collin Brody clung to the little white dog one last time bereft with the thought of not seeing him again until Monday. The pink tongue licked his face and the white dog that captured Collin's heart was gone.

Chapter 15
Joyce

"Mom, I saw a cop coming out of the private room when I picked up Kizzy just now."

Amelia talked fast releasing my sweet dog from his carrying case. He bounded toward me, obviously happy to be home. We had to be at West Point in a couple of hours and the weather didn't look promising.

"Hi, honey. Thanks for being my driver this morning. What's this about a cop?"

"A Lieutenant, no less. In uniform from NYPD. Handsome. He hurried out like a man with a mission. I wonder what that's all about. And Kizzy stayed a while longer until the nurse brought him out on his lead. He had crumbs on his whiskers and didn't tell me where they came from."

I had to laugh. My daughter, the worrier. "He's sworn to secrecy about his therapy work, Amelia. Thanks again. Now you better head home. The weather is changing again." We hugged and away she went.

Bundling up for a brisk walk, my trusty pooch and I walked around the quiet neighborhood. Every old tree had to be leaked on so other dogs knew who lived here. Better than a sign was the stream dogs made to mark their territory. Melting snow created small ponds where blacktop needed repair. Boots protected my feet. When we returned home, several towels were stacked near the front door to wipe my furry pal dry.

My morning had been productive. The final edition of Super Bunny looked just right. A happy ending for small fans to read with him zooming off dressed in his special shirt to reunite with his family. I'd send it to the publisher tomorrow.

Rea Morgan needs more children's stories to illustrate. Bring 'em on. *Mom, are you listening? I've made your name an icon as a children's book illustrator. I don't need fame. All I need is enough fortune to get by.* I set aside Super Geezer just for me. The concept cracked me up. Maybe someday I'd write a book for seniors only and hope there were more of us with a good sense of humor. You need one at this time of life.

My new hip ached today. Barometric pressure or what? We climbed the steps, I opened the door and Kizzy dived into the stack of towels. What a sight! Me, carefully getting to the floor to wrestle my frisky pet before he shook himself dry splattering the walls. Years of experience helped and I won. At last, clean and dry, belly full, he circled three times on a rug near the fire and napped.

As for me, a hot shower and lunch would do it. The trip to West Point took about an hour in poor weather. I loved to see my dog work his magic with Special Needs children and looked forward to this time.

I wore a red sweater for Valentine's Day, applied some make-up, a bit of blush, a splash of cologne and satisfied went to the kitchen to peer in the refrigerator. Slim pickings. A hot dog cooked on my new griddle and five minutes later, lunch. Not exactly The River Club. I paused mid-bite remembering chicken noodle soup getting cold while Collin taught me to play Getting to Know You. I got to know something about him and then his daughter stormed in ending our game. Sadness almost overwhelmed me until common sense jumped in. *Don't go there, old girl. You have a long ride ahead. Literally.*

Chapter 16
Collin

"Edgar, why haven't you married? You've been my right hand man for many years and I know nothing about your personal life."

Edgar glanced up from his book on Albert Einstein. "What leads you to believe there aren't women in my life? Scads of women let alone one." He resumed reading.

"Scads, did you say?" Collin made his way over to the companion visitor chair and sat next to his friend. "You're enjoying some private joke and since we're roommates for the first time in your employment, I mean to uncover your secrets. Speak up or I'll send you out for Scotch and the hospital will put us in lockdown."

Closing his book with a loud thump, Edgar sat tall in his unwrinkled black suit. "Place your hand on this book and swear you will never reveal my secrets, so help you, God."

"I swear etc. Now get on with it. You know how grumpy I can get."

"I did have a wife long ago when you first brought me into your service. Divorce ensued; she disappeared with our two children. A boy, Edgar Junior and a girl, named after the wife, Emmy. I tried to find them to no avail. Time passed, you kept me busy as your company and family grew. The scads of women referred to is an exaggeration. Over the years, maybe twenty and now they've dwindled to about four or five."

"Four or five? I'm astounded, Edgar. Sorry for your loss. Sorry you didn't confide in me back then. Let me get this straight. At your age, mid-sixties, you juggle several lady friends when you're not working?"

Arching an eyebrow, Edgar said, "I do not juggle. Now may I return to reading? I find that Albert and I have a lot in common."

Pacing back and forth, Collin began to chuckle. He pictured Edgar as a juggler in the circus, women flipping through the air around him. Joyce would sketch this for him when he found her. He sat at a small desk in the comfortable room, happy he'd donated the children's playground at Nyack Hospital in his dear Maureen's name. Now in his minor illness, he had a splendid private room with the best of care. Removing stationery from the drawer, pen in hand he made a list of things to do when he and Joyce reunited.

Apologize: beg forgiveness; get down on one knee if necessary. He checked the knee replacement and hit delete. No more on bended knee nonsense.

Joyce is not the kind of woman who requires lavish gifts or is she? His head hurt in the attempt to make a list. An epiphany happened as he sat brains muddled, in a hospital room. *I've been a self-centered man all my life,* he thought. *Yes, I cared for my family and worked hard to grow a successful business but in doing so, I lost a bit of humanity."* Collin looked at Edgar. Really looked at the man who served him as chauffeur, friend, confidante for countless years without complaint and only just now did he think to ask about Edgar's personal life. *I'm like a Scrooge and before it's too late, I'm going to change.*

Chapter 17
Joyce

'Slip Slidin' Away' came on the radio in a Simon and Garfunkel segment on the radio as my car did exactly that on the highway. I clung to the wheel hearing Mickey's voice from beyond say, "Don't fight, go with the spin, then take control." Heart beating as out of control as the car felt, I managed to get back on track. "No stopping for a breath, big boy. You were great this afternoon. We've got to get home safely. Treats, Kizzy." He barked in agreement.

Focus straight ahead as darkness shrouded the road, I watched signs for Palisade Parkway South and heaved a sigh of relief when at last I navigated the awkward turn. Now for the long countdown to Pearl River. Finally the turnoff to Route 304 then Middletown Road and Crooked Hill Road and almost, almost home. At last I gave some thought to the children of deployed soldiers I'd seen today. Their sweet faces responding to my dog always brought tears to my eyes. Mickey and I never dreamed our puppy would be valuable as a therapy dog.

I pulled up the slippery driveway and stopped, hit the emergency brake. Now came the difficult part: carrying the dog carrier in or taking Kizzy out and snapping the lead on before he ran to the nearest tree. Opting for the lead, I opened the latch on the carrier and before I yelled a command to STAY, my dear pooch ran between my legs and marked his territory. Falling hard, I screamed HELP. Like Humpty Dumpty, I'd taken a great fall and slid down to the street. With no one around, I called my faithful companion.

"Come." He came. Just like Lassie, the clever faithful collie in the TV series, Kizzy to the rescue. There are no commands for help me up or call 911. What to do? I reached out my gloved hand and waved it. My smart dog grabbed hold and began to drag, pulling me like a new fallen skater on the icy walk all the way to the steps to my house. He kept tugging until I stood and held tight to the railing. At last I managed to open the door after several shaky tries with the key. Home, warmth, safety enveloped me. I hugged my dog and thanked him receiving many kisses in return. After limping around to open a can of his favorite food, I managed to peel off my clothes and check out the damage. I've found that aging causes skin to become fragile and bruise easily. Not pretty. No more glam poses for me. I laughed. As if someone ever asked for pin-up photos.

Under the harsh light of my bathroom, bruises blossomed purple and red. Of course, I'd fallen on my left side where the new hip still healed. At Helen Hayes Rehab, they warned against falling and said pain would be excruciating if the hip came out of the new socket. A hot shower followed by an ice pack relieved some pain and two Percocet did the rest. I survived to face another day.

We retired early after our adventure. I asked Kizzy if we should move to a warmer climate with palm trees. No icy streets and harsh winters. He barked twice, spun around three times and slept, cozy in his little bed. I'd never leave my daughter and granddaughter and soon, I felt it in my battered bones, Collin and I would be together.

Chapter 18
Collin

Dr. Barry entered the private room for one more check-up before signing off on Collin Brody by eleven a.m. "You're looking well, Mr. Brody. There's great improvement over three days ago. The staff has nothing but compliments for you and Edgar. And your therapy dog has worked wonders from what I've heard." He looked at the chart and laid it down. "Let's get serious about your blood pressure, diet, and giving you an optimum life expectancy." He smiled.

His patient smiled back and said nothing. Edgar moved his chair closer and took notes.

"It's not like you to be quiet. What's up? Something good, I hope."

"Something's in the wind, Doc. My friend with the NYPD has a hot lead on my lost lady. Today might very well be the day I find her."

"Mr. Brody, please don't let your hopes get too high. We don't want your blood pressure to spike again so be cool and let it play out." The good doctor handed Edgar several sheets of instructions and asked him to schedule an office appointment in one month. They shook hands all around and Collin beamed when the door shut.

"Edgar, I'm turning over a new leaf as of today. You are my faithful companion."

"As was Tonto to the Lone Ranger." Edgar almost cracked a smile.

"I have not been a good friend to you and today, that will change." Instead of pleasure and anticipation, Collin observed a look of surprise and fear on his manservant's face. "What?"

"Please 'don't change a hair for me, not if you care for me.' Up until now everything has been just fine. You're generous, good to be with, respectful of my privacy. I want you to be in good health, find your lady and all of us live to a riper age."

"That's from a song, My Funny Valentine."

"Indeed."

"Edgar, we will find her. And thank you for your kind words but Damnation, I'll do as I please."

"You always do."

The phone rang. Larry O'Brien calling. "Collin, I'm on the way to this address on Paul Court in Pearl River. Cora is with me just in case we've found the right house and Joyce opens the door. I'll advise ASAP."

"It's happening. I feel it in my bones. First a quick shower and shave." He limped to the bathroom flinging his cane aside whistling My Funny Valentine. "My dog is due here very soon." Collin shouted through the closed door. "Lay out some clean clothes. Um, please."

Always way ahead of demands, clothes were on hangars ready to wear. Edgar muttered, "He's not your dog, boss."

Exhausted by the simple act of everyday actions, Collin laid down. "Just for a short spell, Edgar. I feel weak, no energy." His eyes closed and he slept. *Maureen came to him as she sometimes did with a hint of lavender, her favorite scent. Time to begin a new life, my love. Take care.* He inhaled her scent and slept on.

Chapter 19
Joyce

"Mom, sorry but you'll have to take Kizzy to Nyack Hospital for the last visit to their VIP patient in a private room. Ask for Nurse Randall at the front desk. The room number is 409."

"Oh. Okay. I have to make myself presentable, if at all possible, and brush my teeth and my pooch. What time?"

"Ten a.m. and you can't be late. Uh, Mom are you all right?"

"Fine, honey." *Nothing a new body wouldn't fix.* No need to worry my kid. I peeled the shell off a hardboiled egg salted, followed by a piece of toast lathered with marmalade for a quick fix. Teeth and Kizzy brushed, I did the minimal touch of make-up. Adding blush to my cheeks and fresh lip gloss, I felt good to go. I made my way carefully down the sanded steps and in the car with no mishaps. Kizzy grinned a doggy grin and I made my way to Nyack Hospital. Mickey died there. A night never to be forgotten, now placed in my memory bank as I moved on one foot in front of the other.

Route 59 turned out to be an easy twenty minute trip east and I followed the signs making a left and a few blocks up took a right into parking. Taking Kizzy by his lead, I strode in with attitude, to the front desk giving the room number and stating my purpose as therapy dog owner. Immediately I received a pass and followed the signs to the elevator. Carrying my precious cargo, I rode to the designated floor, again following signs to the room.

A tall solid nurse with an authoritative manner blocked my way.

"I'll take the dog in."

Ready to punch her one if she stopped me, I said, "No disrespect to you but this is my dog. I've trained him as a therapy dog since he was young. It's my place to take him in to patients. I have years of experience and a license to prove it. So please step aside." She did, with reluctance.

I knocked and entered.

Familiar with the scent in the room, I smelled lavender, and the patient, Kizzy twirled around on his hind legs in a display of pure joy. Releasing the lead, I watched him jump up on the hospital bed and lick the sleeping man. Collin Brody. My Collin. His blue eyes opened. He blinked, stroked my dog in just the right way and beckoned to me. I moved close to hold his hand so warm I tingled down to my toes.

"Joyce? Oh, Joyce."

"Yes, it's me."

"And Kizzy?"

"He's my therapy dog. I've had him since puphood. He trained to."

"Hush for now, my lovely lass. There's so much for me to tell you but first forgive me for ignoring you on our first date."

"Hmm. First date, was it? Not satisfactory. Do you want a second chance then?"

"How many chances are you willing to take?"

Edgar slipped out of the room.

The phone rang. "Collin, Larry here. It's her house all right. An old Cape Cod style. #23 on the mailbox. Campelli mail inside. I knocked at the next door neighbor's house. He said we just missed her. She had her dog Kizzy with her. That's your therapy dog's name. I don't believe in coincidence."

"She found me, Larry. Tis a miracle. I expected one last visit from my therapy dog this morning before leaving the hospital and got more than that. Thank you, my friend, for your effort and love to Cora. Actually you found her too, right on time. We must celebrate. Good bye."

"Larry and Cora O'Brien? How in the world do you know them?"

"'Tis a long story, my love, about a foolish old man and his quest to find a lovely woman. Truth be told, 'twill take years to tell."

Chapter 20
Once Upon a Time

"And so dear children, that's the whole story of how we met twenty years ago."

Clouds darkened the winter sky as if they too knew the story ended for today. "More, Grams, tell us more." The grandchildren clapped their sweet unlined hands. Lindy ran over to hug me. "Grumpy's sleeping."

"He catnaps often. I'll cover him. Please do your Pied Piper routine and get everyone in for dinner. Miss Mary is ready, I'm sure. As ever, she prepared a feast with your favorite dessert, crème brulee. Roast beef at the carving station, red roasted potatoes shaped like mushrooms, broccoli, steamed spinach and sautéed button mushrooms and..."

"Tiny chocolate chip cookies and so much more. What a love. Thanks, darling Grams. See you inside."

Always careful not to fall, I tapped my way to Collin with a cane in one hand. His hand felt icy cold to the touch. Fear clutched my heart. Rubbing gently to warm his hand, I spoke to my beloved. "Are we beyond sleep, Collin?" my tears spilling on his clean shirt.

Faded blue eyes twinkled up into mine. "Are we finished telling The Story?"

BEFORE THE
FINAL CURTAIN

by
Charmaine Gordon

Dedication

I say this again and again, where would I be without the firm guiding wisdom of my publisher, Kimberlee Williams? She's taught me more I ever dreamed of about writing books. I'm proud to be a part of Vanilla Heart Publishing.

A special shout-out to Chelle Cordero, my personal anchor woman who has literally shown me the way many times and anchors me to reality.

Acknowledgement

Here's to what I lovingly refer to as "The Sweet Time" in my life; when I moved from wife and mother to fly by myself, drive to NYC, take classes, join unions, audition and actually work.

Writing *Before the Final Curtain* brought back fond memories of that time and to always remember, never cut funny.

Enjoy the journey, dear reader.

Chapter 1
Introducing Becca Morgan
fading actor of Broadway acclaim

"Home at last." Becca Morgan set the cat carrier down after flinging open the carved oak door to her home overlooking the Hudson River. Freeing her faithful companion from his prison, she laughed as he meowed and bolted for the litter box. "Good idea, Jack. Are we happy or what?" Becca almost skipped to the master bedroom wheeling her bag. Inhaling fresh aromas from her own home after three months on tour in the Mid-West filled her with joy. Sarah, her housekeeper forever, had cleaned up, tended the garden, used lemon polish to make every wood surface gleam and best of all, Sarah left homemade pasta sauce to cool on the butcher block counter.

She stretched out on the queen sized bed. "Mmm, lovely to be home." Gazing around the spacious room Becca took in the awards cabinet in all its' glory. Polished Tony's, Emmy's, Golden Globes and plaques—tributes to past performances. Tears trickled down her thin face no longer young. *Get over yourself, Becca. Starring roles aren't written for seventy year old women. No more. Not since Katherine Hepburn.*

Now for a hot tub to ease my aging bones, she thought. Becca stripped, opened the sliders, towel and cell phone in hand to remove the cover. A few buttons pushed and instant bubbles greeted her. One toe in tested the heat. Becca settled in to soothe aches from hours of travel.

The cell phone shattered the peaceful moment with her favorite tune, Happy Days Are Here Again.

A quick dry with a towel and she connected.

"Becca." Her heart beat a little faster in recognition of the voice. Randall Sloan, the powerful director she'd worked with many times in the old days when he was called Randy apropos of his philandering.

"Randall. So nice to hear from you after too long a time."

"Becca love, I've written a new play perfect for you. I'll FAX the script right over unless you're not interested." He laughed, a smug familiar sound that hadn't changed.

Fingers crossed, she said, "Don't tell me my character is the faithful companion or the housekeeper."

His voice deepened to a sexy growl. "You're the lead. Titled "Honor Thy Mother, Please", a poignant comedy, small cast."

"The lead? Oh, Oh, Oh. What's the part?" Naked outside on her veranda, Becca wanted to dance, sing, shout out loud.

"You'll have the script shortly. We bring it downtown in a few weeks to a festival in Chelsea and then midtown off Broadway and finally Broadway."

"You know me, Randy. I can't wait. Not even for a few minutes. Please tell me about her and what happens." She knew he loved to be begged.

"Oh, all right. Here's a taste. She's a lonely widow who lets her daughter and son-in-law move in with her. They abuse the privilege, treat her as if she's no longer capable so when they're at work she goes to a bar and meets a man. Just one more thing, Becca."

"And what might that be?"

"Are you still in good shape?"

"Good shape? Why do you ask?"

"Your costume in part of Act One is a towel."

A towel. Not much sagging at seventy since she exercised daily. The little castanets under the arms were too difficult to keep firm. No biggie. She had the starring role.

Thanking God for big opportunities Becca tried to play it cool. Like another day, another starring role. Then she bubbled over. "I've kept in shape, thank you. Sounds wonderful, Randy. I'm excited. I just returned from a tour of On Golden Pond in the Mid West and I'm so ready for New York." She gave him the FAX number and raced to her small office to watch pages of a new script drop into the tray ready to change her life. Fingers itched to highlight her part, memorize and above all to prepare. Skimming she realized she forgot to ask about her leading man.

This called for a celebratory something. With no one around but Jack, her old black short haired cat with green eyes that followed her all day and Playful, the Hermit Crab purchased while on a romantic tryst at Cape May Point safely in her tank with all the other Hermies, they'd share a cup of rice pudding.

"Jack, we've been on a long journey together. You, Playful, the kids, Mom and Dad are my constant in life. Back to the green rooms again and this time, we're in New York. No traveling for a while, I hope."

Jack wound around Becca's legs impatient. When she opened the pudding container and placed a generous dollop in his dish, he hunkered down and purred, pink tongue lapping. Becca Morgan also purred eating every drop before she got to work. *Meow, you old cats out there auditioning your hearts out. I'm the new leading lady.*

Chapter 2
Introducing Christopher Williams
at home in Mahwah, NJ

Hollywood sucked the juice right out of me, Chris thought. *A year there, One movie, three potential pilots with promises of series, too much booze and silly women always ready for the casting couch. And stupid me. Big money made but it's so great to be home.* After two weeks with no calls, bored out of his skull, Chris walked out to the neglected flower garden to dead head petunias. Pinching each one with such ferocity, he almost missed the clarion call of his cell phone.

"Christopher, old boy."

"Cut the crap, Randy. I don't like the word old. It's one of the few three letter words I've eliminated from my vocabulary. You called because."

"You're the same endearing guy who busted my chops on stage and off. Most actors are thrilled to receive my summons. I have a part for you."

"How big, when and where?"

Randall Sloan laughed. "As usual you cut to the chase. Leading man in my new play."

"Leading woman?"

"Becca Morgan."

Long silence. Chris's rapid breathing slowed.

"We haven't worked together in a long time."

"True. It's magic time again, Christopher. Give me your FAX number and you'll have the script in a few plus a schedule."

Chris peered into a mirror after what should have been an extraordinary high from Randy's call. "Mirror, Mirror on the wall, what the #@%&#!happened? Years, that's what and too much Hollywood foolishness. At seventy three, he needed to be fit and energetic to perform the heavy schedule demanded in New York. Better than ever. And Becca. His one and only. No woman touched his heart the way she still did.

He concocted a veggie/fruit drink, added an egg to the blender and drank. Good and so good for you said the ad. Uh huh. Dusting off the treadmill after removing clothes tossed, carelessly thrown as if it were a hanging rod, he walked slowly at first and picking up the pace, he ran. Stopping for water and the script, Chris sat on his stationary bike to nowhere set at medium pace for thirty minutes and rode while he scrutinized every word and pictured every scene. The one where the main characters realize they may have a future together moved him to tears. His lines did it. *"Once smooth without a scar or blemish is not possible. This is life. And we show the marks of experience. At the end, no one leaves the wrapping as smooth as we came in. Look past my scars and see my heart. This is my unblemished gift to you."* Chris squeezed his eyes shut when he finished reading in hope of tears not falling on the wonderful script. They did, like tiny raindrops. He examined his emotions. Touched, amused, charmed and then some. He showered, checked his steamy image in the mirror again. An improvement greeted him.

A plan formed in his actor's mind. *Picture this*, he thought. *We see each other across a parking lot where the Drama Bus is parked. Randy always hires a Drama bus for the cast. The ensemble waits. I stride toward her fast, rejuvenated. Oh shit, old man, you ain't what you used to be.* He sucked in his gut gaining height and straightened his wide shoulders. *Think positive and go for a ten. Becca Morgan, here I come.*

Then Chris began the real work, highlighting lines, memorizing as he turned pages. Cramming the words into his memory bank over and over until he slammed the script on his desk and shouted, "Yes, I can!" No one came prepared with lines learned like Becca, damn it. This time he wanted to at least make a good showing at the read-through. *In bed with her, back in the good old bad days, we'd go over lines and let them flow. If I'd stumble, she'd calm me down. We can do it together, she'd say. All past tense.*

"You're not in bed with her, yet" he said out loud and picked up the script. "Learn the first page. Pretend her warm body is next to you. Feel the heat, the love and the lines will come to you."

Three hours later, Chris nailed his first scene.

Chapter 3
Meet the Team

Always one to arrange the gathering with style, Randall Sloan had what he call The Drama Bus pick up everyone who didn't live in New York City at a designated central location, Exit 5 on the Palisade Interstate Parkway. The Bus, a large station wagon had the capacity to carry four actors, a stage manager, the assistant to the director, and the costume designer all in comfort. They met in the free commuter parking lot about the same time.

Jane Nelson, a sturdy middle age woman stood feet planted apart, clipboard in hand. "Gather around, people."

Penny Cranford hurried from her Toyota, bag in hand bumping against endless legs. Tall, blond hair long straight and shining, she had her first big role as Becca Morgan's daughter in a new play. "I'm so excited," she said to no one and everyone.

"Hey Penny, We made it. Good to see you." Brad Joseph moved in close to his soon-to-be stage wife. Also tall, handsome with slick dark longish hair, Brad and Penny made an attractive couple. "This is great."

The costumer, Selma Leon observed and made mental notes. Beautifully dressed to keep up her image, a mauve chiffon scarf tied casually around her neck floated in the slight breeze. Selma, an old timer in the business, had worked with Randy many times and had awards to prove it.

The assistant to the director, Jimmy Corcoran staggered out of an old VW with a stuffed battered briefcase.

"Selma, hi it's me, Jimmy. I was your second in the last show."

"Nice to see you, uh Jim."

"Ms. Nelson, I'm moving to an apartment, well a one room thing down near 4th Street so I won't be on the Drama Bus next week. Just a heads-up." His face turned red with the lack of interest. *Someday, before too long,* he thought.

Chris Williams sauntered over, leather bag slung over a wide shoulder, a bouquet of red roses in his left hand. "Hello, everyone. Let the games begin. I'm Chris Williams." The young actors shook hands with Chris. He planted a kiss on Selma's cheek, and hugged Jane. He made a point of striding toward the disheveled young man and introduced himself. Learning Jimmy would be assistant to the great one, he knew the kid must have talent. Then he looked around. "Where's Becca?"

"Making a grand entrance as we speak." Jane pointed her pen to a black Mercedes pulling up.

"That's not like her, Jane." Chris strode toward the woman he'd dreamed of for years. She stepped out of the car, slim as a girl, blond hair layered shoulder length, wearing a chic summer dress in a raspberry color. Accepting the roses and a kiss on the lips, Becca allowed Chris to carry her bags to the bus. He kept talking, she listened.

Penny watched. "I'd give anything to know what he's saying."

"Not your business. They are stars with a history." Pen in hand, ready to check off names as if this were a cast of a huge musical, she bellowed. "Welcome to The Drama Bus. Before you board, you may call me Stage Nazi just once. That's all you're allowed. After that you may call me Jane."

The kids laughed and mumbled Stage Nazi. "This is totally cool. I love it."

"You sound like a Valley girl, Penny. From this moment on, get in character. Sit with your stage husband, Brad and run lines. There's no time to waste."

Brad took Penny aside. "Jane runs a tight show from what I've heard and she watches out for behavior infractions. Heaven help any actor who doesn't have lines memorized within one week and perfectly. No paraphrasing allowed."

Penny whined. "No paraphrasing? You must be joking. What have I gotten myself into?"

"A hit Broadway comedy, baby. Don't blow it."

"How is Playful?" Chris grinned, his teeth sparkled like a sunny day.

He stopped Becca with his out-of-the-blue question. The Hermit crab he bought her years ago still lived to remind her of a reckless love life. Now she lived a hermit's life, kind of. Quiet even when she worked on tour or daytime dramas or made for television movies. Considered to be on the B list at her age, still great but more someone's best confidant, once cast as a nun, twice as a madam.

Her laughter filled the air enveloping them in the old cocoon they'd spun to protect them from gossip mongers. Back in the day photographers followed the golden couple, gossip columnists wrote about them and eventually marriages dissolved. In the parking lot together they shimmered interrupting each other, word spilling and all about a Hermit crab that captured their fancy at Sunset Beach. Four dollars and ninety cents plus the little carrying case, plus food, plus a larger shell when she outgrew hers. "Girls need a new outfit", Becca said. More laughter.

"Playful lives?"

"Oh yes and she has many Hermies for company. I bought a glass tank for their comfort and safety."

"These roses are for you, Becca."

"Well, thank you. How, hmm, nice."

They walked toward the waiting entourage as if it were a stroll in the park with no pressure.

Chapter 4
The Drama Bus ride

Extending a slender hand, Becca introduced herself to her stage daughter and stage son-in-law. They fawned over the star who smiled in her gracious way. She hugged the staff with genuine joy and stepped up into the bus, greeted the driver, Dan O' Brien and floated way back to a comfortable seat for two.

Chris followed the plan. Cast partners sat together and ran lines. All business this time. He slid in the seat close to her. She didn't blink those long lashes, a good sign.

"Did you notice Randy kept our real names as characters in the script?"

"Yes, Weird, don't you think?" Sunglasses removed in the air conditioned bus, Becca turned full face to her once lover. Aware time had taken a toll on both of them, she whispered. "So here we are again. A little older and maybe a little wiser?"

"Older, yes. Wiser, I don't know. We had a lot of fun, Becca."

"Chris, I know where the bodies are buried. We hurt our mates. What happened to Sylvie?"

He chuckled. "She married before the ink dried on the divorce papers. Dear Sylvie was having an affair with a guy in our building. A widower with a couple of young kids. It worked out for her and we keep in touch once in a while. How about Harris?"

A long sigh almost told the story. "Sad to say he came out of the closet, went wild and acted foolish. He got AIDS and died."

"Did you know he was gay?"

"No. From the day we met, Harris was gentle and kind and a sweet lover. Our sex life was satisfactory until," they gazed at each other, "until you."

Chris touched her hand. "That's very sad, Becca. I had no idea. Are you comfortable moneywise?"

She flashed an impish grin. "I'm great. Harris left me a bundle." A change of subject before she revealed too much. "We're stars again. Let's work."

Out came the scripts. Becca used a yellow highlighter; Chris used blue. "And away we go."

Chris read: The play begins with a lot of action, background mumbling, moving furniture as a bewildered Becca stands stage left watching her belongings brought downstairs to the lower level of her home. Her daughter Laura and son-in-law Max are moving in and taking over.

Chris laughed at the first line in the play. A great sign.

Becca: "Basement? I don't live in the basement."

Laura: "It's not the basement, Mom. It's the lower level."

Becca: "So why don't you live there?"

Laura: "Mom, we need more room. There are two of us and."

Becca: "Thanks for reminding me, honey. I almost forgot your daddy died."

Laura: "And Max needs space for an office. It will be just fine, you'll see."

Becca: "He can use the shed, the garage, the attic."

Laura's not listening. Forlorn, Becca sits on a couch. Movers lift the couch with Becca looking hopeless as she's carried downstairs.

"Wonderful beginning. Funny and touching. What's your opinion, Chris?"

"I love you. I mean I love it. As you said, funny and touching. The kids take over, she's lost and has to find her way back when she goes to a bar and meets me. The hero. I do love you, Becca."

"More bullshit, Chris? I'm not into anything but truth."

"The whole truth and nothing but, dear heart. You'll see. Before the final curtain, you will know."

"Hmm. Let's work on our scenes, lover boy."

At the front of the bus, Penny and Brad sat side by side listening to Jane Nelson's rules.

"From now on you are Max and Laura, husband and wife taking over Laura's mother's home without thinking about her needs. Laura," Jane turned her intense brown eyes on the young woman, "you believe your mom is no longer capable of doing much so she can be bossed around without considering her feelings." Jane included the two actors. "You both work. She's lonely at home and restless. You have no idea she's gone out and met a man at a nice hotel bar, think Ramada. Two mature people without partners stranded in a never-never land of life. Unaccustomed to drinking, she orders a Chardonnay, sips half and he restrains the pretty stranger from climbing up on the bar to tap dance.

Laura appeared to be breathless. "And then what happens?"

"Laura, did you read the script? All of it?"

Red faced, Laura shook her head. "Do it." Jane turned her back to Penny and walked away steady as she went down the aisle to sit with the grown-ups.

"She's right, you know. We have the opportunity of a lifetime. I'll help you if you reciprocate." Brad moved in closer to his cute actress partner.

"Thanks, Brad. I will." She sniffled, close to tears. "I need more discipline."

Selma Leon, renowned costume designer, thought about the young woman playing Laura. Notes in her book. Too young. She's supposed to be about thirty, a working woman. Instead she's early twenties, hot, sexy. How to age her? It's going to age me working with a twit like her. And why did Randall cast this kid? Must be the casting couch. He's gone through enough of them to keep a furniture store in business. Bet he gets a discount, the randy old buzzard.

Jane slid in next to her, read the notes and nodded in agreement. Any hope? scribbled Selma. Jane shook her head. "I doubt it. Brad looks right. The director is using her. They don't call him Randy for nothin'. We'll see about Blondie. She can always be replaced by someone more appropriate. Like someone who can act and chew gum at the same time."

167

Jimmy Corcoran opened his briefcase and began to organize. Assistant to Randall Sloan, a huge break for him, Jimmy was determined to be successful and make a name for himself. With his parents' approval and a little financial support, he had big plans for this play. Always known for being a funny guy in school, writing skits good as Woody Allen everyone said, yeah right, he'd put his talent to work.

Chapter 5
The Read-Through

Greeted by the big man himself at a small theater on 35th Street, excitement grew. A tray of bagels, cream cheese and assorted fruit set on a side table attracted attention. Actors' appetites, like their personalities, were always ready to be nourished center stage.

"Let's get to the read-through as soon as you set your bags aside. Note pads are on the table, folks, scripts out. In ten minutes, we're on." Jane watched the small ensemble move in place, satisfied for the moment. She poured coffee; one for the director, one for herself and sat, timer in hand.

A timid Becca entered already in character for Act One. She had changed from her lovely summer dress to a plain dark cotton old thing packed for the occasion. Always the consummate performer, Becca was ready.

Read through became a stumble through with the young actors trying too hard to make a good impression. "Relax," Randall said many times. "Read the lines. They're right in front of you." A ten minute break for food and tears and they resumed. Becca and Chris lived their parts without looking at the script, pauses in the right places, comedic timing in every scene perfect. Applause around the table. Becca requested a meeting with Randall and Chris.

They went to her temporary dressing room. Blue eyes flashing, she shook her head. "Randy, first for some unknown reason, you use our names as stage names. I don't get it. Second, you know Chris and me from way back and you've written this wonderful play about us. Without asking. What the hell?" She turned to Chris. "Do you recognize us in the story line or am I paranoid?"

The director sat, legs crossed and watched his stars in action.

"Honey, yes of course I see us in every line and the play is wonderful as you said. But here's the rub. I see nothing wrong with Randy writing it. Shakespeare said, There's nothing new under the sun." So why not?"

Becca stomped around the small room, dust motes kicked up in her wake. The men waited allowing her to think it through, live with the inevitability and at last, give in.

"My name should be Maddie. Chris, what's a good name for you, the lonely bachelor?"

Chris pondered the question. "What's in a name? How about Kevin?"

"Kevin, Kevin, Kevin. Sounds good. Nice."

"Maddie and Kevin it is."

Randall Sloan stroked his beard and nodded.

True to Becca's nature, she wet a clean cloth at the sink, patted her face and washed her hands. Finally she smiled. "Let's get back to work."

At the next break a caterer showed up bearing yet another tray of food. Happy murmurs of thanks from the always hungry cast and crew. Chris indicated to Becca he wanted a private chat. She steered him to her dusty room as an icy feeling came over her. Years before he'd do the same thing like play director and tell her how to deliver a line. *Not again, please not again,* she thought. *Make love, not war. It weakened her ability as an actor, cut into her self esteem. Actors are fragile.*

"Is there a problem?"

He grinned his charming way of indicating no problem here. Becca knew him so well and he hadn't changed no matter what he told her. "The line in Act Two after we've made love the first time. You say, "I can't believe this happened." Don't be so upset. Say it more in surprise. It will get a big laugh."

"Really? You're the expert, the director here?" She wanted to hit him upside his arrogant head. "Did you do that in Hollywood, Chris? I'll tell you for the first and last time, don't direct me. Have you forgotten that's why we broke up years ago? You have a mean streak." She stormed out of the shabby room.

At her response, Chris reached out to touch her. Pulling her arm away, she said, "Lovers on stage only. I can act the part."

In the ladies room she ran cold water over her wrists. *This is a read-through and already there's conflict between us. How am I ever going to survive?* She gazed in the old mirror and liked her reflection. *Not bad for an aging broad. Of course I will. Broadway here comes Becca Morgan again.*

Head held high, she sailed back to the stage, pausing for a miniscule taste of bagel with cream cheese. "Thanks for the food, Randall. I'm ready whenever you are." She flipped through pages of the script, reread the line Chris referred to and thought, *"He's right, the bastard. Why is he always right?*

Chapter 6
Rehearsals

Penny and Brad stood awkwardly center stage as the director dressed them down, a job usually left to the stage manager but at this point one week before the festival in Chelsea, Randall Sloan's hair stood on end.

"I cast both of you out of a large group of hopefuls and you are letting us down." He paced back and forth, shaking his head. "We don't have stand-ins, people and I don't want to audition anyone. All I need is energy, involvement, react and act. Take it from Scene 2."

Max: Where's your mother?

Laura: Sleeping. She's lonely, you know. I've tried to get her interested in sewing circles and cooking lessons.

Max: She's a terrible cook.

Laura: Don't I know it. When I was a kid she'd ruin a jar of pasta sauce and spaghetti by cooking it so fast the pasta was still stiff and the sauce was cold. Dad loved her. I think she still misses him.

Max: She should get out, meet someone, get laid.

Laura: (hits him with a pillow) Max, you're talking about my mother.

Max: Sorry you're right. She's too old for romance. C'mere baby. I'll make nice with you. Don't worry about your old lady.

"Better. Pace is good. Please continue with the scene keeping in mind there's a sexual aura, humor, and lack of understanding about the mother and love between you. Bright, I want bright " Randy gave thumbs up to Jane.

When he left the room she'd get after the kids. Too sloppy with dialogue in her opinion. She crossed her arms on her ample chest not satisfied.

Becca listened, felt the loneliness of the mother, the loss of her husband, the sexual part of her husband gone forever. Ready for the scene where she tells her daughter about the traveling salesman husband who returned and couldn't wait to have her on the floor, couch, sometimes they made it to the bed. She loved the lines about to be spoken.

Scene Three

Maddie: Your father was a traveling salesman, you know.

Laura: I didn't, Mom.

Maddie: Oh yes. He'd come back after two weeks so horny, we never made it past the front door. He just dropped his suitcases and his pants and"

Laura: Mom!

Maddie: And sometimes the couch, bless his heart. Later on we'd get to the bed. When I sold our possessions I should've kept his. Oh, never mind.

Laura: What, Mom?

Maddie: His suitcase. He had lots of toys for us in there. Always something new. Never should've sold it. Lots of good memories.

Laura: Oh, Mom.

A short scene, applause and everyone laughed, tears in their eyes at Becca's reminiscence done with a straight face and Penny's shock at the thought of her parents having a sexual life.

"Perfect," Randall applauded. "Penny, you had just the right reaction to your mother's story. Becca, superb. Move on folks. Jane, take over. I have some calls to make."

Chris walked toward Becca , a gleam in his eyes. She turned away, not willing to accept his critique. He held up a hand. "Please allow me to say one thing. You did justice to a difficult scene sitting in a chair without much expression, you captured my heart. Again. Thank you."

With a nod of her head, Becca acknowledged the extraordinary compliment from her co-star and heart skipping just a beat or two, she sat.

Satisfied the rehearsal went well, Randall dismissed the cast and asked the staff to remain.

"So, what do you think?"

Jane, always the first to voice her opinion, spoke up. "Penny needs work. To say the least. Brad's good and improving."

Selma handed over sketches to the director. "First of all Penny's a problem. She's too young to be playing thirtyish so I've had to age her up. Take a look. Regarding Becca, her dress worn on read-through is perfect. Dowdy, just right. I'll have my seamstress make a few more. Then I've sketched a progression; one for the hotel bar and then a pretty dress for the end. About the towel. Randall, it must be a big towel or a blanket. Which one?"

"Big bath towel, please and off white."

She made a note. "About Christopher. He needs to look a bit dumpy at first. Hard to do since he's great looking. I think a loose jacket, ill fitting, brown with brown trousers and brown scuffed shoes. Spiffing up as his confidence grows into blue. And now Brad. Slicked back hair because he's a know-it-all, loose tie, rolled up sleeves, striped shirt, jeans. Like that.

"Thanks, Selma. You're a wonder. Bring everything in by Friday, please." Meeting over, Randall Sloan sat alone in the darkened theater.

Usually the casting couch brought good results to the stage, he thought. This time he had doubts. *I need a perfect cast to get back on top. To cut and cast someone else at this late date or give Penny one more chance? The festival in Chelsea would be his barometer.*

Writing is rewriting. Randall grimaced. Did Shakespeare rewrite? Probably not. All the world's a stage and we are merely players or something. With lines like that tripping off his tongue, scripts poured from inky fingers.

He'd convinced backers, his agent and a new producer with connections who wouldn't interfere. Always a gift of gab, his mother bragged about her youngest son. Too bad she hadn't lived to enjoy his success. In private he reread his beloved script, noted where a line might be changed or added, a process he followed until opening night.

Chapter 7
The Drama Bus Ride Home

Becca sat in her own world after the exhausting rehearsal. Up the West Side Highway across the George Washington Bridge in heavy traffic, eyes closed. Quiet on the bus. Chris sat apart from her just the way she hoped he would. Space necessary between them. Scenes from their early years played out like a twisting kaleidoscope. They met in a musical, The Apple Tree. She played Eve with five solos. Delicious voice back then. Gone for good now. No more musicals for her. Chris couldn't sing but neither could Rex Harrison. A script to die for and Chris her leading man, Adam. A man to love. Over and over they were cast as couples on stage, coupling back stage. Scandalous. They were married but not to each other. Show business. You forgot real life. How stupid.

Across the aisle Becca heard Chris humming, "Look at you, look at me," as if he read her mind. One of her songs from The Apple Tree. Their eyes met. They smiled at each other. Past and present collided. Becca turned away. Home in twenty minutes and peace.

A can of Fancy Feast cat food opened and mashed in his bowl and Jack forgot about her. Now Becca had what she called "Me Time." The music of Ray Charles played on DVD; she poured a half glass of Chardonnay into a crystal wine glass and dined on a glorious avocado and shrimp salad Sarah left in the fridge. Stress faded with day's end. The Hudson River never looked so splendid with sailboats heading this way and that. "Safe journey." She toasted the sailing enthusiasts with another half glass of wine, Chardonnay her favorite.

All thoughts of the play were gone. Almost. Chris' comments good and mean sometimes drifted back. Damn. He's haunted me for years. An old song came to her. "You go your way, I'll go mine; it's best that we do." *Yes. My theme song with him. From now on, keep my distance and only connect with the play.* In black marker she wrote those words at the back of the script.

Sleep came easy to Becca Morgan once she'd made a plan. Not so with Chris Williams. Entering the old house in Mahwah inherited from his grandparents, loneliness came over him. No kids, no wife, especially no Becca. Again he'd screwed up any chance of connecting with her. Only on stage, she'd said. They were harsh words and he deserved them. He looked in the fridge, and wrinkled his patrician nose and selected reduced fat peanut butter and no sugar apricot jelly. Cutting off a touch of mold on whole wheat bread, he walked out to the garden where dead headed petunias flourished and he ate. Gourmet dinner for a star. An apple for dessert sounded just about right.

Visions of Crème Brulee, Filet Mignon, steamed spinach, and red roasted potatoes danced in his head. Ever the optimist, he'd square things with Becca, if possible, and they'd fine dine before long. Gossip columnists, photographers get ready. We're back.

Penny showed up at Randall Sloan's posh apartment after freshening up. She flew into his open arms. After some heavy romancing he poured champagne and talked business. "Sweetheart, we have work to do. Take it from the top." He barked orders, directed, caressed her until Laura began to evolve into a real person speaking words that rang true. Then he released her, both of them weary. She went home in his limousine. Randy elated with his success, poured single malt Scotch into a shot glass, drank a toast to Viagra and finally fell asleep.

Restless, Brad Joseph stopped at his favorite bar for a beer and burger. A few buddies called him over to ask about work, always a hot topic. *Time to brag a little*, Brad thought. *Not too much.* He spun his chair around to straddle nice and easy. "I have great news. You know I've been taking classes, auditioning and staying afloat by working as a waiter." They all nodded and leaned forward. "So I got this big part in

Randall Sloan's new play!" "Way cool" and "When?" were some of the responses and before long the whole bar cheered for one of the gang who made it.

Jimmy Corcoran rewrote a scene in Act One. Not completely. He didn't want the old man to freak and throw him out. All he did was what writers called tweak to make dialogue more believable and natural. First, he'd show the new lines to the stars to get them on his side, nice and friendly. If they bought them, maybe they'd make the move. Jimmy squeezed the writing pencil so hard it snapped. *There's nothing like a little tension, Jimbo, to keep you on your toes.* He didn't want to blow a big chance.

Chapter 8
Dress Rehearsal

Costumes pressed, Selma presented them on a rack on stage, each one labeled. This moment excited everyone; the morning was spent trying on, fitting, pins to adjust if necessary. Accustomed to dress rehearsal activity, with assistance from Molly, the seamstress, Becca changed behind a screen from a moth to a butterfly, in Selma's words.

"Thank you for all the work you've put into these costumes." Becca twirled around in the final scene pink dress falling into Chris's arms. He caught her as she tripped, not the light fantastic, but by a loose floor board on the old stage. Then dipping her in a graceful dance movement, they bowed. She pulled away. "This isn't in the script."

Jimmy called out, "Maybe it should be. It's so romantic and funny."

Chris glanced at his dancing partner. "He may be right. It felt good and this play is like a coming-of-age for us, romantic with a big splash of humor." He peered over the footlights to see the frowning director. "Randy, what's your take?"

"Hmm. Let's see it again. From your line before."

Kevin: You are beautiful in and out of that dress, Maddie. It's time to." (Maddie twirls, Kevin catches her as she trips, they dip and bow.)

The company laughs and applauds. Standing ovation.

"Good idea, Jimmy. Thanks." Becca, always ready for new lines and stage directions, knew Randal would be bent out of shape. Pouring two mugs of coffee, she added sugar and walked down the stairs to Randall with his steaming drink. "Hey big guy, Jimmy added to your wonderful script. That's what we're all doing to make this a hit. Each little schtick rings true so open your heart, okay?"

Her favorite director took a big slurp of the sweet brew and allowed a smile. "You're right. It's scary when the young ones come up with good ideas, isn't it?"

Becca sighed. "Right now all I am is grateful to be the leading lady in your new play. One day at a time, my dear. One day at a time."

Penny whined that her costume made her look too old. "You're supposed to be close to thirty, Miss." Annoyed, Selma tried to be patient. "I designed your costumes for you to be age appropriate and they are perfect. I've been in the business longer then you're alive so trust me."

Brad whispered, "Shut up, Penny and stop complaining. You look perfect."

"Take it from the scene where Laura is worried about her mother not being home." Randy leaned forward from his seat in the audience to watch how his girlfriend de jour would perform.

Laura: I'm worried about Mom.

Max: What's the big deal?

Laura: She's never out this late.

Max: Take deep breaths.

Laura: You idiot. She's my mother.

"Excuse me." Jimmy raised his hand.

The director said, "Another country heard from."

"Uh, How about if Laura says, "You idiot, I'm not in labor, I'm worried about my mother." And Max says, "While she's out, let's do something about getting pregnant." And they reach for each other and forget about Mom. Lights out."

"Oh" Becca clapped her hands. "Another good one, Jimmy. I like it."

"Ten minute break." Randall Sloan rose to stretch. ""New blood."

Jane, the Stage Nazi, nodded. "Sometimes we have to make room. As much as I hate to be territorial about every word you've written, I admire your attitude, my friend. Surprised yet filled with admiration. Who'd a thunk it?"

"Actually, I'm going to kill him. Jimmy," he roared "come."

Like a whipped dog prepared for another beating, Jimmy cowered before the tall director. Just when he thought he'd gotten away with adding his precious two cents into the script, he was up the creek without a paddle.

"I took you on as a favor to your decent parents. A favor, do you understand?"

Jimmy didn't get it. "But I thought you liked my work and figured I'd be a help. You did a favor? Oh my God." He crumpled into the closest chair. "I'm embarrassed and I'm a fool to think my ideas had merit to add to your excellent script.

Assuming the role of sympathetic mentor, difficult for him, Randall said, "The protocol is to speak with the writer first and in my case, I'm also the director." He sat back in the chair next to the young man and rubbed his hands together. "Jimmy, do you have any other ideas you wish to share?"

Perking up, Jimmy almost spilled the contents of his bulging case carried everywhere. "Uh, Yes. Sure, Mr. Sloan and thanks for being so understanding." He slid out the latest notes, grabbed a pen and pointed. "This is from the bar scene where Kevin and Maddie are getting acquainted."

The director closed his eyes and pictured the scene. A hotel bar, she's just taken a sip of wine, he makes a tentative move and asks her name.

Kevin: My name's Kevin. What's your name?

Maddie: I'm not telling.

Kevin: Why not?

Maddie: My husband's a sniper with the local SWAT team.

Kevin: (almost spills his drink) Oh. Sorry. (He begins to move away)

Maddie: (she touches his coat sleeve) Just kidding.

"What do you think, Mr. Sloan.? Is it funny, good or what?"

"Hmm. I see possibilities, young man. Let's keep our conversation private and if you can do that, we'll add this and any other ideas you tell me about, always between us, in the script. Right now, type it up, make copies and hand them to Chris and Becca. They are quick studies. Afterward have lunch. Break is almost over."

"Something is rotten in Denmark." The stars met privately in Becca's soon-to-be-replaced dressing room when they moved into a different theater. "First Randy's assistant comes up with some great additions to the script. Then the all powerful director takes him aside for a serious discussion and next we're handed some really funny new lines."

"And you believe the honorable, and I use the word loosely, Randall Sloan is taking the kid's work to pass off as his own."

"Yes, I do. Jimmy Corcoran is getting shafted."

"It's not the first time. Back stabbing is part of the industry. There are decent people and there are sleaze balls. As long as we do our work, the play's the thing."

She kept her distance from him, never quite trusting the long ago lover. Hurt me once, shame on you; hurt me twice shame on me. The old saying held true. "The new lines are funny."

"Yeah, Jimmy has talent. Shall we run lines?"

She pictured the scene, set it in her mind. "Go."

"My name's Kevin, what's yours?"

She burst into laughter. "I'm not telling." "This is so comical. A seventy year old woman acting like a kid. You said we're coming-of-age in the storyline and I hate to admit it. You're right again."

Chris moved closer, his hearing aid needed a new battery. "Did you say,I'm right again?"

"Yes. Uh, Chris, didn't you hear me?"

"Damn. I thought I could keep it a secret." He lifted his longish dark hair up from one ear to expose the appliance.

"Since when, Chris?"

"Last year. So far the other ear is all right. Hey," he grinned. "it's not cancer."

An instant reaction to his words caused Becca to cry. He'd touched a nerve.

"What?"

When his arms enfolded her, she nestled her head under his chin reminiscent of the old days. "I'm a survivor, Chris. It was awful but here I am."

"Here we are."

Warning bells sounded in her heart. She pushed him away. "I can't take a chance, remember? Lovers on stage only."

He left so quickly, a chair fell over.

A quick trip to the restroom to use Visine for red eyes and the pat of cold water over her wrists. Good to go.

Ever present Jane bellowed, "Breaks Over. Everyone on stage."

"Take it from the top, new lines, in costume, clock is running. When I say Scene, begin. Lights out. Scene.

Utter chaos as everyone did their best and at the end of all the stumbling, the director said, "Not bad. Now do it again."

Chapter 9
Micro Managing

With the leads gone home, Randall smiled. He surveyed his two pliable young actors. "Usually I don't micro-manage but now is a good time. The bedroom scene need beefing up." He saw them deflate like two balloons stuck with a pin. "No, don't despair. Think of it like a touch up of roots gone gray." Not the analogy for young people but what the hell. A chuckle from the exhausted actors. "Okay. You've just made love and Max is ready to roll over and sleep satiated. Laura's thoughts return to her mother. She pokes him in the back.

Laura: We shouldn't have made her sleep in the basement.

Max: Mmm. What?

Laura: I'm talking about Mom. She allowed us to move in and now she's gone. (She cries)

Max: (reaches for Laura and they begin to make love)

"Scene." Randall shouts. "What we need to bring the audience into the story is for you to take the moment before so take it." They look blank. "Climax. When you make love, feel it. The earth moves. Shudder in the glory and hold each other as your bodies quiet before you, Max, roll over to sleep in peace. After a piece. Let me see it."

In a tangle of bodies under the covers, Max and Laura kiss, acting urgency became reality. Moans of ecstasy emanated from the darkened stage. Staff and crew leaned forward, voyeurs to the scene Randall wanted.

"Scene."

Max: Oh, baby. (takes her in his arms) She's old. She doesn't need a big house. How about a dog? Let's get a dog for her.

(Laura slugs him with a pillow" Go to sleep. I'll figure something out.

The small audience laughs, applauds.

"Beautiful." Randall, pleased with his genius, moved on not paying attention to the caresses going on between the young actors.

Chapter 10
Whose play is it now?

Jimmy existed on pizza and juice each day after rehearsal. Overhearing comments about the improvements in the script and how Randall was at the peak of his career caused him grief. In his fourth floor one room walk-up, he sat on the floor temper boiling. He picked up the pizza box and hurled it against the wall to watch sauce and pepperoni slide down. *What a mess*, he thought *and I'm the one to clean it up. Always the one. The fixer. My words. My script. When will I ever get credit? Scrubbing turned the wall a nice shade of pink. His writer's mind churned and a scene formed.*

Scene Two Act Two

Maddie: I can't believe this happened.

Kevin: Did you enjoy it?

Maddie: Yes, but

Kevin: Kissing?

Maddie: Yes, but

Kevin: Touch?

Maddie: Yes, but

Kevin: But what, my dear?

Maddie: My, uh, butt hurts

Jimmy rolled on the floor laughing. "I love this," he shouted.

A neighbor banged on the wall. "Shut up in there or I'll call the cops."

Probably runs a meth lab in the bathroom, Jimmy thought. *Gotta get out of here and soon.*

"My play will preview in Chelsea at a competition festival. We are going for the big win, people. Randall strutted around the stage as Jimmy handed out new scenes. "Read and memorize. We have no time to waste. Autumn leaves will start to fall. We want to open on Broadway as soon as possible."

"Easy for him to say. New pages every day." The kids grumbled.

Becca and Chris read their new scene. They called it the butt scene and loved it. "Jimmy is so talented. The play improves with every page he writes. The secret is out."

"Agreed. And he probably won't get credit." He shrugged. "Not this time. Next show it's all Jimmy and we'll be asking to have parts. Read through?"

"Of course."

They read cold then added nuances and timing and the fun began. Yes, but became a private cue to laugh.

Over iced tea, Chris became talkative. "How are your parents? They must be in their nineties about now."

After a deep calming breath, Becca flashed a smile. "Thanks for asking. They're in good health. Dad just slowed down in his law practice allowing the younger partners to work harder. Mom won first prize for the best key lime pie again. That's twenty years consecutively, a lot of blue ribbons."

"Did you inherit her love of cooking?"

"Guess not. Sarah's been with me for many years. She's in charge."

"Sarah?"

"My housekeeper." *Trapped. She hated the feeling. Secrets led to a complicated life. Lie upon lie. Not for her yet in this case one BIG FAT LIE! Becca didn't want to go there, not with Chris.*"Sarah's the chief cook and bottle washer at my humble abode by the river." *Not too bad and all true so far.*

"What river, where?"

"Chris, you're asking too many questions." She stood ready to run and hide. "My turn. Fresh air is what I need and now."

He almost fell off his chair. "You know actors are never allowed outside."

"I. Need. Fresh. Air. Got it?"

"This is the city, Becca. Open the doors of our air conditioned theater and you get pollution, fumes, exhaust.

Fresh is where your mysterious humble abode is. Fresh is Mahwah, New Jersey where I live, not far from you, Ms."

Jane's voice boomed out. "Places."

"Let's play hooky."

"Hey Chris, we're stars again. Don't you love the feeling?"

He pinned her to the wall, lifted her chin and they kissed. Light and sweet at first in harmony. Her arms raised to hug him around the neck. "Oh Becca, I've dreamed of this moment for years. He pressed his body closer and lifted her skirt.

"Places for Scene One Act Two." The voice of Jane Nelson demanded attention.

"To be continued?" Chris released his hold on her. Against her better judgment, she nodded.

After rehearsal, Jimmy Corcoran got up courage to speak to Becca. "Ms. Morgan, may I talk to you in uh, like private, uh just for a minute?"

"Of course and please call me Becca. Come with me." She led him into her dressing room. "I'll be happy to leave this theater tomorrow. Sit. What's on your mind?"

Better at writing than making conversation, he blurted words she never expected to hear. "I know your kids from high school and just realized it. Charles looks exactly like Mr. Williams and Beth is the image of you. I went to private school in New Hampshire, see, and it just hit me."

Her face lost all color. Worst fear come true. What to do?

"Ms. Morgan, uh Becca, I upset you. Huh. So nobody knows, right?" She nodded. "Not even Mr. Williams?" Stricken, she nodded. "Giant secret to keep and I'm sure you had good reasons. I've watched you and you're the best of everyone. Kind, thoughtful."

"A regular Girl Scout, Jimmy."

"And funny." He put his hand over his heart.

Tears streaming unabated, Becca thought, "*Oh no, he's going to pledge allegiance.*"

"I will keep your secret, it's a promise."

"Thank you, Jimmy. I've carried my secret for a long time and for many personal reasons. I'll be revealing all to Chris and my twins before long. When I'm ready. And I want you to know I'm going to push Randall Sloan to the wall to at least get you on the playbill for credit. You have talent. Your parents will be so proud." On tiptoes, she reached up and kissed him on the cheek. *Someone else knows. It's up to me now.*

Chapter 11
The Chelsea Competition

Cheerleader of one, the great director stood before his cast, staff, and crew in the small theater in Chelsea, host to the competition. "Please get your cell phones or communication devices out and call everyone you know to buy a ticket for Honor Thy Mother, Please. It's all about votes. We've done great work with rehearsal, the script aided by Jimmy Corcoran, my able assistant, and no disruptions. I'm talking fist fights, tantrums." Everyone laughed, tension broke.

"Four plays: Our beauty is Mature Romantic comedy/drama, one is serious drama-spare me from too serious, please, another is sci-fi—don't ask. I haven't a clue, and last a small country musical—also no clue. Critics will be there. Pay attention to no one except the play and all we've worked for. Broadway is set no matter what. I have a producer, backers, the theater. Not to worry. Go for a ten. Remember to take the moment before and the audience will be with you. Let them feel, love, connect."

The group applauded, standing O for Randall Sloan and the lighting people went to work setting scene by scene. Sound professionals tested the system and worked with audio. High ceiling meant good acoustics. Behind the scene were the pros who enhanced the play to its' fullest.

Chris changed the battery in his hearing aid and made sure he had a supply of fresh ones in the backpack. Sometimes there was a feedback if he didn't push the aid in all the way. He shuddered at the thought. Checking it twice, he felt the pressure perfect, passed one hand across his ear and no squeak came out. He breathed a sigh of relief. *The golden age is not so golden after all. Oh well. I'm a star again.*

Shared dressing rooms were a pain. He expected privacy and wondered why this damn preview in Chelsea. Publicity? There must be money involved or Randy wouldn't do it. Brad strolled in, hung up his wardrobe and grinned. Kids. At that age, Chris had already starred in a bunch of plays with Becca as his co-star. Lovers and friends. Until he became bossy, overbearing, and as she said, mean. The End. He wanted to begin again. But first the play. Concentrate, take the moment before. Sitting with eyes closed, he became Kevin.

Watching the star, Brad knew he would learn from him. He sat in the other chair

and closed his eyes to take the moment before. Absorb the script, make the scenes with Laura personal. Gone were friends, auditions, old girlfriends. Brad became wise-ass Max.

Chatting away, Penny waved to a soundman and slammed the dressing room door she had to share with the star. "Hi." She spread out items from her cosmetic bag and threw her clothes bag across a chair. Becca glanced up at her, no expression on her face. "You must be kidding. Move your belongings to one side of the counter and hang your bag in the closet. And be quiet. This is quiet time. Get into character time. Don't you dare screw up everything we've all worked for." Becca closed her eyes and became Maddie.

Chastened, Penny did as told. Yes, she'd worked very hard subjecting to the advances of the great one. And now she'd found sweetness with her co-star Brad. *Grow-up, girl. This is your dream come true so don't blow it. You've wanted this since you were a little kid.* Penny sat, closed her eyes and followed the lead of a major star. She became Laura.

Chapter 12
Curtain up; light the lights

Out front the full audience rustled programs, settled in seats, chatted and laughed. Backstage the actors focused, calm and quiet, Becca sipped a drop of Chardonnay her doctor prescribed to steady her voice. And the recommended breathing most actors used . In through the nose for a five count; hold for five; exhale for five through the mouth. Worked wonders.

Honor Thy Mother, Please was the last play on the agenda. "Places," Jane called in a stern soft voice. The four actors held hands for half a second. Each took the moment before and they were on.

How glorious the feedback of an audience. A bond formed with each scene as the audience laughed and fell silent listening to the wonder of actors living a story before them. At the end, when Chris and Becca danced, dipped and bowed, the audience leapt for a standing ovation. Over and over again, applause. Flowers were handed across the footlights to Becca and Penny. A new hit in Chelsea soon to be on Broadway. A call for the writer/director. Randall Sloan dressed in a tux, stood and bowed. To the cast's surprise, he gestured for Jimmy to join him. "My assistant, Jimmy Corcoran, who added to the script." Shy, young and happy, Jimmy waved to the cast and audience and hugged the famous director.

Exhilarated, the cast left the stage as volunteers dressed in black walked through the audience to collect votes. "We'll meet after we change. Down at the bar where the winner will be announced. *Winner,* thought Becca. *Get us to Broadway. We're ready.* She changed to a pretty scarlet dress with sparkles all over, long sleeves, high neckline. Ballet shoes to match. Hair piled high on her head, she twirled and almost lost her balance. *Again. Hmm. Something to be concerned about.*

Penny emerged from the ladies room dressed in a slinky black sequined dress, slit way too high with towering heels. *Oh my,* thought Becca. *Bye, bye Randall.* "Aren't we lovely. Someone once complimented me by saying after a play, Death of a Salesman, I cleaned up very well. And we do."

A giggle from Penny as she almost fell off her heels. "Let's go down together. United we stand. Divided we fall. Right?"

"So true." Arm in arm they made their way to the elevator through the crowds and compliments, smiling. "Fame can wear you right out so always remember to nap when you can and nap alone." Another giggle from the young actor and down they went to the bar.

The head of the Chelsea Foundation, George Weiss, called for attention. "We have the winner of our twentieth Chelsea Foundation Competition. Drum Roll, Please."

"Is there a play titled Drum Roll, Please," Becca said and her cast, crew, director, everyone went crazy with hugs and kisses. "What?"

"We won. You missed the announcement. We won. Broadway, here we come." Chris scooped her up in his arms and kissed her, kissed her, kissed her.

"Oh, Chris. Here we are again."

"Yes. Take me to your mysterious humble abode tonight, love. This very night."

She had to tell him. The kids were coming to the opening on Broadway soon enough. One look and they'd all know. Be strong and confess tonight.

"There's sure to be a party tonight."

"We'll go. For a while and duck out."

"Car? We're both parked at Exit 5 on the Palisade."

"Hmm. Cab to Exit 5 and I'll follow you anywhere."

 "Let's get our bags from upstairs and head to the party, wherever. Ask Randy."

In the elevator, Chris said Randall would host the party at his apartment overlooking the Park on 52nd. "Nice. We'll meet the producer, backers, the money people. This is exciting."

"Not as exciting as the party afterward." He whistled a happy tune.

Tingles went up and down her spine with the thought of making love with Chris after all the years. Her skin had changed. Little brown spots or mole thingy's were appearing daily. Dermatologist needed or what? And she had scars from cancer surgery, faded now but they were in intimate areas. No man had been naked with her since Chris. And her shoulders were kind of bony. Nice inventory. *Old girl, I told you before, get over yourself. You're not the young girl he met years ago. And he's not the young man. So what? Love and be loved.*

Randy went all out with his party. Penny prowled the room leaving no man untouched. Chris and Becca held hands and presented themselves as older versions of the way they were. Fawned upon by important people is what counted at the party. The producer, Sam Reiss and backers, a husband and wife team, Bill and Gwen Barry were enamored of show business and theater. The soon-to–be lovers stayed much longer than intended because Randy insisted.

As the guests began to leave, Chris and Becca did, too. They snuggled in a cab all the way across the George Washington Bridge to Exit 5 and Chris found it difficult to walk in his condition. "It's not my back, baby, it's my front."

"Too much information. Follow me."

Chapter 13
Secrets Revealed

Chris kept up her pace in the warm evening, a full moon overhead guiding their way. *Time's almost up, old girl. Before or after the love. Before became the right answer.* Pulling into the driveway, she heard loud meowing. "Poor Jack. He's hungry. I have to feed him first."

Nervous, she dropped her keys and Chris held her hand steady as she picked them up.

"The river is so close. I hear the water against the rocks."

"There's a hot tub on the deck. We can strip and go in. It's wonderful."

"You're wonderful. I love you." With nothing to stop them except her conscience he lifted her in his arms to kiss again and again.

"I have to feed Jack or he'll drive us crazy." Opening the door, she hurried for the cat food. Jack stared at Chris, green eyes narrowed. When he heard the bowl touch the floor, he scampered to dinner and forgot about someone he once knew when he was a kitten.

"He's spry but old."

"Kind of like us, Chris. Come see Playful." She lifted the big Hermit Crab and set her on the floor. The crab lumbered around and hurried to visit Becca. "She thinks I'm her treadmill and likes to run up and down my arms."

"An old Hermit Crab."

"They live long lives if they're taken care of and have company. Very Playful."

"Like humans."

"Yes. Oh, yes."

She stripped fast, left her clothes on the bed and before he said anything, Becca ran outside and turned on the hot tub.

Two towels on the bench and she settled in the bubbling heated water.

"You've done this before. No fair." Chris made his way slowly to the tub and slid in beside her. "I had to take my hearing aid out before getting in the water." He glanced around at the view. "Spectacular. The sound, water, no one to spy or is there?"

"Not that I know of. Wine?"

"Half a glass of white, like you."

She reached near the tub where a small fridge held wine and poured two glasses. "I have something to discuss with you before we go further."

"We're sitting in a hot tub starkers and you want to talk?" He hugged her close and clinked glasses. "There's something I've wanted to ask you, darling. Did you ever regret not having children?" He looked out at the river peaceful and calm, voices of youngsters laughter carried across from somewhere.

"Oh Chris." Tears flowed like the river below. She wanted to shrink from his gaze. "Hang on tight, love. Here it comes. Remember way back when I took a year's hiatus from the stage saying my parents needed me?"

A far-away look came over him. "Yes, yes I do. We missed out on a great play that year, and I couldn't reach your agent or anyone connected with you."

"That was the year I became a mother." Heat inflamed her cheeks.

Chris almost choked on his next words. "You have a child?"

"Two, actually. Twins. A boy and girl. Well, they're in med school. Doctors both. No dramatic arts for them."

"Harris's children?"

"Oh, Chris. It was all so long ago. You may recall I was on the Pill but I had a bad cold and took antibiotics and somehow that negated the Pill's protection. That's how I got pregnant. Well, having sex a lot did the job."

"Harris's children?" he asked again.

"By then, you were my only lover."

"I'm a father? How could you have kept this from me?" Anger flashed in his dark eyes.

"Chris, you always said you never wanted children and it was an accident. I didn't want to burden you, to ruin your career with a scandal."

He cut her off. "How old are they and how sure are you they're mine?"

She turned off the bubbles, dried her hands and reached into her carry bag, fished around for pictures always there. With loving care, Becca lifted the small portfolio and asked Chris to dry his hands. He did. Handing the pictures to him, she couldn't stifle the sharp intake of breath when he first gazed at a mirror image of himself at who obviously was his son, the daughter a miraculous blend of both parents. "She's beautiful. All the years wasted." Faces pale in the moonlight, they stared at each other. Becca knew Chris needed time to absorb her revelation and she wondered if in telling him, she'd opened Pandora's Box.

"You know your line, "I can't believe this happened? In Act Two?" She nodded. "That's how I feel right now. Who do they think their father is?"

"I wrote unknown where the birth certificate asked for father. My parents don't know. They never questioned paternity. They asked no questions when I showed up at the door, a homeless waif. Just took me in, helped raise the babies who call them Poppa and Mumsie. After a year, I returned to New York and traveled back and forth as much as possible. I had the freedom to resume acting and we kept it very private, easy to do in the spacious area where they live. I helped financially although Dad always made money with his law firm. And I hired a nanny to help. They went to private school in New Hampshire later on. Oh, they're twenty seven."

"Twenty seven. When can I meet them?"

"Opening night?"

"No. How about tomorrow or Sunday. Please, Becca. Make it happen." He stepped out of the tub, pulled her with him and dried her naked body first. "To the bedroom. Enough trauma and breaking news for one night. All I know is you did what you believed to be best for me. I didn't want children. I remember saying those words. What a fool. And now we begin fresh. It's not the end."

"Is it the beginning?"

"Yes. And that's a promise." Chris gathered Becca in his arms carrying her to the bedroom. He locked the sliders; she pushed a button and Rogers and Hart's Where or When sung by Frank Sinatra filled the room. "We've stood and talked like this before,"

"Naked," Chris interjected. She blushed.

Sinatra sang on. "We looked at each other in the same way then but I can't remember Where or When."

"The clothes you're not wearing are the clothes you didn't wear before," Chris sang off –key, with a sweet grin.

"You're incorrigible, my love. My only love for too long." Becca reached for vanilla body lotion on the night stand, poured some in her hands and used long lazy strokes to soothe Chris's arms. "Do you like?"

"More, much more." Stretching out next to her petite body made him aware of her delicacy, cancer she'd survived, secrecy of their children. "Pass the lotion, sweetheart. I want to pleasure you." With each stroke, he placed a kiss. The lower he went, the more erotic their private scene. His hand felt the smooth skin go to irregular and stopped. "Cesarean section?"

"Yes. Don't look too closely. The old gray mare, she ain't what she used to be."

"You are like fine wine, sweetheart. Aged to perfection." Chris continued his path down to find more scars where he smoothed lotion and then the portals to heaven. "May I? and didn't wait for an answer to touch and kiss his dearest in the intimate way they'd taken for granted. Delighted in her response of a gasp, he rolled on top. And she yelped, NO.

"I mean, try this. Becca grabbed a fancy purple pillow and shoved it under one hip. "Okay. Now carefully try that maneuver again because honey, up 'til now we're doing just fine."

The hours went by as they found a different way to make love without hurting each other's aging bones. The sun came up; lovers slept on until his love barometer woke up. "Not again," Becca sighed in mock horror. "Oh well, we'll do it until we get it right. Take 5, Roll camera. five, four , three , two, Go."

After a very late breakfast, she called the twins and confirmed an early dinner this very day. "Ask Sarah to make a lot of food, Mom. We're hungry," Charlie said. Beth chimed in with, "he's always hungry."

In a panic, Chris paced through the house. "Hey, this humble abode isn't so humble. Harris did leave you a bundle. Your trophy wall is fine, so full of memories and then we lost touch and went separate ways."

"You must have quite a collection, Chris. What did you do with them?"

"Nothing." He shrugged. "I moved so they're still in cartons unbroken, I hope. Let's see what's for dinner and make plans. What'll I wear etc."

Hugging him, she said, "You can borrow my yellow Halston dress."

"That's a line from Tootsie. You're like an elephant. You never forget."

"Look who's talking. Now regarding food, Sarah must have a sumptuous dinner in the fridge. Let's check."

Holding hands, they almost salivated at the feast ready to go. Everything Chris dreamed of in fine dining. Four Filet Mignon's seasoned to grill, roasted red potatoes ready to heat, steamed spinach casserole fifteen minutes or microwave at four, according to a taped note, and Crème Brulee. The note said use flame thrower two seconds to crisp. Bon Apetit. Sarah."

"Wait a minute, wait a darn minute. How did your Sarah know there would be four for dinner tonight."

"Magic, I guess. She's like that."

Chapter 14
Family Ties

Four o'clock on the deck, Chris swallowed two Tylenol with water to ease a headache. *I'm a father. It's a fact. And twins are coming in a few minutes. Will they like me or think I'm a fool for not taking care of their mother. And them.* He rubbed his forehead, checked for the tenth time to feel if the hearing aid stayed in place. Blue chambray sleeves were rolled up to look casual, jeans fit okay, Chris finger combed his hair and chimes rang. He turned, almost fell over when a Chocolate Labrador Retriever barreled into him, jumped up and slobbered kisses on his face.

"That's Gracie," Charlie Morgan said.

Wiping his face with a once clean sleeve, Chris said, "Goodnight, Gracie."

A beautiful girl, the blend of Chris and Becca, said, "Goodnight, George" and they all laughed.

"So you must be our dad."

"Ya, think, Charlie? Just because he looks like you or rather you look like him? Smart uh. Sorry, Mom. I almost cursed."

"Let's sit." Gracie sat at her favorite command. She wagged waiting for a treat. Charlie gave her a small biscuit and rubbed her back. "On the deck. Beth, please bring the tray with people treats out and all of you can get acquainted. Make yourselves comfortable. We are family even though this is an unusual circumstance."

When they were settled in comfortable chairs, Gracie on a big pillow next to Chris for some reason known only to her, Becca began. "I want you kids to know none of this is Chris's fault. He never knew I was pregnant because I left New York claiming my parents needed me. The reverse was true. Chris always said, please kids, remember we were young, in love and popular on the Broadway stage, he never wanted to have children His career came first. As an only child from divorced parents, families didn't mean a whole lot to him."

Charlie raised his hand to speak. She asked him to wait.

"Also we were married but not to each other. Foolish. Things happen. You get involved in a play and forget real life. There's no excuse. So I disappeared to have you and re-appeared a year later to resume my career. Traveling back and forth to help care for my babies, I hired a nanny to help Mumsie and sent money to establish education plans for both of you. Chris and I never worked together again." Becca took a moment to breathe in the clean fresh air she loved near the river. "Last night I confessed to Chris he is your father. Beyond surprise, he absorbed the news like the gentleman he always has been. And that's the whole story, children."

"So what are we supposed to call you?" Charlie popped a crisp bacon wrapped shrimp in his mouth and chewed with a little hum, his habit since babyhood

"Hmm. My name is Christopher; most people call me Chris. I'll leave it up to you." He selected the same appetizer also chewing and Becca noticed a hum coming from her lover. She smiled.

"Thanks for finally coming clean, Mom. I like Dad. I always envied everyone who had a Dad. Even my friends with divorced parents had a couple of Dads."

"And Moms. Don't forget the plethora of stepmoms, grand moms, real moms at our last graduation. Too many to count."

"At least we had Poppa, Mumsie, Mom and Nanny Francis. Better than most of the screwed up families."

"Yeah. So would you mind if we try Dad on for size? See if it fits?"

Chris bit his lip in an effort not to cry. Becca squeezed his hand. "It's okay, dear. They're exuberant to say the least and don't bite your lip. You need it for the play."

The men inhaled the snacks. "I'll start the grill, Mom." Beth unfolded her long legs and almost made it to the kitchen.

"Allow me. I saw a griddle in the kitchen. That should work." Chris plugged it in, turned up the heat and pulled the steaks from the fridge. "Please follow the directions Sarah left so everything will be ready at the same time."

"Roger that," and soon father and daughter worked as a team.

"Mommy, do you love him, our new real dad?" Charlie laid his head in Becca's lap.

She smiled down at him stroking his hair so like Chris's. "That I do, my son. That I do. Don't blame him. I'm the one who kept secrets. Best to be open and you won't have regrets. I'm guilty of robbing my children and my lover of twenty seven years. I have to live with that. He said a funny thing when we talked about age last night. He doesn't buy green bananas anymore. There's no time to waste."

"Mom, Sis and I forgive you. Really. We've lived in the coolest environment all our lives with one component missing. And now he's here. Will you marry him?"

"I just might do that. But first I have to propose and see if he accepts." Mother and son decided to see what the other members of the family were up to. Gracie slept on oblivious to the drama around her. Jack hid under the bed, green eyes watching the big dog.

Charlie finished dinner first as always a member of the clean plate society and pushed his chair back. "Since you are stars accustomed to drama, I want to present a new play. Reality style. Judge and jury. Mom, you are accused of withholding important information to the health and well being of your children. How do you plead? Guilty or not guilty?"

"Guilty, uh Your Honor." She choked on a small piece of steak. *What was he up to?*

Beth jumped in the game. "I'm her lawyer, Judge. My client is not guilty. She was a young woman torn by obligations not wanting to ruin the reputation of another famous Broadway star with a scandal. I submit to you this evidence," she handed her napkin a few pieces of spinach clinging to it, to her twin, the Judge. He studied the cloth, removed fragments of food and refolded it.

"The jury will convene 'til after dessert." With elaborate ceremony, Charles ignited the flame thrower and one by one, lit each sugar coated Crème Brulee. Then he blew out the fire and served.

Caught up in the imaginative way their children were acting out, Chris could hardly wait to see the finale. Young med students with actors blood in their veins. They'd make fine doctors.

"Does the jury have a verdict?

"Yes, Your Honor." Beth poked Chris. "That's your one line, don't blow it."

"Yes, Your Honor.

"What say you?"

"Not guilty in any way. Becca Morgan, my dearest and only love, marry me and make these innocent children legitimate."

"Way cool." And "Awesome" from the twins.

"I do. I mean, I will. I love you, Christopher Williams."

Chapter 15
Opening Night on Broadway

"Places," Jane called. "And you can refer to me as Stage Nazi after all we've been through. You're the best troupers I've ever commanded. A ripple of laughter in the green room, the clasp of hands and the cast took places.

Becca had given her words of wisdom speech to the younger cast members before Jane called places. "Never glance at the audience. You don't want to have anyone distract you, take you out of character even for a nano-second. A third wall exists between the actors and audience. Don't lose sight of it. When you look out to deliver a line, you're thinking inside your head or speak and turn to your partner just as you do in real life. This is basic, kids. Easy to forget. Essential to your craft. We've come a long way together. I've loved every moment." She gave dangling earrings as a gift to Penny, a gold chain to Brad, and her heart to Chris who lounged against the wall with a thumbs up gesture and a grin.

From Becca's opening line: "Basement? I don't live in the basement," the audience was captured. Penny became the thoughtless daughter and each character developed just as Randall, with a lot of help from Jimmy, had written his wonderful funny, touching play.

When Becca tripped, the audience gasped. Chris caught her, they danced, dipped and with a grand flourish, bowed to the audience, the response was immediate. A standing ovation. Whistles, applause continued. The stage went dark for a minute. Max ran out and bowed followed by Penny. Chris took his turn and at last the spotlight hit Becca. She bowed, held her hand out to Chris. They bowed together and the young actors joined them. Over and over the curtain closed but the applause never stopped 'til finally it was over. At the final curtain, flowers were handed up to the women, "Author," people called and Randall Sloan rose to the occasion knowing he'd reached the pinnacle of success. Again.

Backstage the twins, Becca's parents and admirers packed the hall. "Everyone out," Jane called. "Thanks for your attention but it's a fire hazard having so many of you back here. Please wait outside. It's a nice evening. Hang on to your wallets and handbags. You're in New York City, folks."

"Jane, our children and my parents are coming to my dressing room."

"Of course." Jane watched the elderly couple and two kids in maybe their twenties follow Becca. And Chris. *Did she say our children?* Jane wondered. *Not her business. Much.*

"Mom, Dad, that was awesome. What a great play. I bet it runs for a long time." Beth sat at the make-up table and tried on different shades of lipstick.

"Beth's right. We couldn't stop laughing at the yes, but scene. Poppa thought that was hysterical and Mumsie had to smack him 'cause he almost choked from laughing too hard. Maybe I'll go into Geriatrics as a major."

"Iced tea, everyone?" Becca poured small glasses half full. "Let's toast to the success of Honor Thy Mother, Please and to our soon-to-be wedding. Chris and I have decided to make it legal."

"Well, it's about time, young lady," Mumsie said. Carefully with a slight tremor in aged hands, they toasted the couple.

"I'll be flower girl."

Charlie pinched his sister. "I wanted that job."

"Nitwit, you can be ring bearer."

"Okay."

"Have they been smoking something or are they always like this? I'll have to teach them some manners. Bedside manners for doctors, Dummy Edition." Chris enjoyed the give and take fun he'd never had with siblings.

"Darling, they're always like this. Better than fighting. We must all settle down. Critic reviews come out and that will tell the real tale of success. We have to attend a party for a short while. You're invited, kids. Poppa and Mumsie, we can get a limousine to take you home if you're too tired to attend the party."

"Nonsense. Wither thou goest, we must go."

"It's settled. We have a limousine courtesy of the director. I'll change into something suitable and off we go."

"Mom, am I presentable?" Beth wore a simple black short dress with pearls and spike heels. With her young body, she looked perfect.

"Honey, all the women there will have cleavage to the nipples and skirts slit to the crotch. All that glitters is not gold. You will be refreshing in the cloud of haze presented among the razzle dazzle crowd. I have this dress," she pulled it from the wardrobe, "simple, elegant, black with a touch of sparkle in the fabric designed by a friend who wants to be recognized. Only my back is exposed. Do you like?"

"Thanks, Mom. Good advice. And I must borrow the dress sometime."

"Very nice dress, Becca. I must borrow it soon." Mumsie sipped the tea without a spill.

"Take a number, my favorite girls. Tonight's my night.

Chapter 16
A Thanksgiving Wedding

The groom said, "All set?"

"All set. Did Jane call places?

"Jane's not here. Just our children, Gracie, your parents, Sarah and the Justice of the Peace. Not even my agent."

Becca stepped out of the dressing room wearing an off white suit with a lace shirt. Hair loose around her shoulders, Chris thought once more she looked like the young girl he'd fallen in love with years before. Heart thudding in his chest, he placed her hand inside his jacket to feel the beat. "This is our beginning, sweetheart."

"Yes, Dearest. Not the end. Do you have the script memorized?"

"Of course. Places," he said and grinned.

Flowers adorned the long table. The small audience sat; the Justice of the Peace had a faint smile on his somber face. He had seen the actors in many plays and now in the intimacy of the home over-looking the Hudson River, he was privileged to join them in marriage. But first a performance.

Where or When sung by Lena Horne played in the background. Chris began."Picture this: A young man cast as Adam, a young woman cast as Eve, fell in love just as the character did in the play. Art and life collided."

Becca said, "Their paths parted as we know." She sang, "You go your way, I'll go mine, It's best that we do." "And years later they reconnect to find love lost and found. So my darlings, Chris and I ask you to join us in our Beginning. Justice, we're ready."

Flower girl Beth scattered rose petals; Charles patted his jacket pocket where the rings were safe.

After the short ceremony they were pronounced legally married in the great State of New York. With gold rings on their third fingers left hand, a champagne bottle cork popped and Gracie chased after. Sarah's quick hands saved the beautiful tray she'd prepared. Dressed in jeans, she never expected this to be her friend's wedding day. Becca apologized for her negligence, found the sweetest dress for Sarah and fixed her hair in a quick up-do. All her favorite people in the world gathered on this special day.

Thanksgiving had a special meaning this year. Many toasts, many tears for love lost and found. Clean plates thanks to Beth and Charles. Becca's parents did the best with small portions. And Becca and Chris held hands under the table making slicing turkey difficult. They ate sweet potatoes and some delicious cranberry mash Sarah concocted. All they wished is for their loved ones to be gone. Like bye bye and take care. See you later. But no. The party lingered on and on 'til at last the newlyweds were alone.

Waving goodbye, Chris picked up his bride and carried her over the threshhold, right through to the bedroom where he placed her on the king size bed. "Places, Mrs. Williams?"

"Yes, Mr. Williams."

And so it began.

More Great Books by Charmaine Gordon

The Catch
Tom Donnelly, once known as The Catch – every woman's dream guy, has fallen down every rung of the ladder he once worked so hard to climb. On New Year's Day, he realizes just how far he's fallen, and makes a list of resolutions to change his life. He vows to regain the trust lost from his family, his law firm, and his friends – and maybe even find the right woman this time.

Sin of Omission
A twist of fate intervenes when Shelley keeps a secret that threatens to break apart the Costigans and her future. A mysterious client, Deanna Rose, enters Haven, victim of a savage beating under strange circumstances. Shelley investigates and finds Ms. Rose has an unsavory past. With the reputation and safety of Haven at stake, Shelley is at risk to lose everything and everyone she cares about.

Reconstructing Charlie

Charlie Costigan has a secret. Home life gone from bad to the worst when she protects her mother from another vicious attack by her drunken father. Midnight. Clothes thrown into an old suitcase, she races for the bus with a letter to an unknown aunt and uncle. "This is my daughter. Embrace her as if she were your own." Determined, Charlie begins again. Alone with her secret.

Now What?

I held his cooling hand and asked the two words spoken many times during our years together. "Now what?" This time there was no response. I was on my own for the first time. When my fingers touched his wedding ring, I slipped it off and held it in my fist. The gold band was warm. I clung to him. "Come back to me, dearest." Sometimes what you wish for is more than you can live with.

Starting Over

Each morning, Emily Kendrick runs on the hard-packed sand of St. Augustine Beach to clear her mind and heal her heart. From the widow's walk of the house perched high on the dunes, a man trains his binoculars on Emily...

 **ALSO IN AUDIOBOOK!**

To Be Continued

Elizabeth Malone wakes up the morning after an amazing night of passion with her husband of forty years to find a note: Dear Lizzie, it's not you, it's me. Abandoned by her husband, disappointed in daughter Susie's casual attitude Dad's having a mid-life crisis, Beth decides to re-establish herself as the winner she once was. When Frank Malone returns, he's in for a big surprise!

Charmaine Gordon writes books about women who Survive and Thrive. Her motto is take one step and then another to leave your past behind and begin again. Six books and several short stories in three years, she's always at work on the next story. The books include *To Be Continued, Starting Over, Now What?, Reconstructing Charlie, Sin of Omission* and *The Catch*, just released.

"I didn't realize at the time while working as an actor in NYC, I'd become a sponge soaking up dialogue, setting, and stage directions. I learned many tools of writing during the years watching directors like Mike Nichols and actors including Harrison Ford, Anthony Hopkins, and Billy Crystal. And would you believe, I was Geraldine Ferraro's stand-in leg model, my first job giving me entrée into all the Unions needed to work. When the sweet time ended, I began another career and creative juices flowed."

You can reach Charmaine at
http://authorCharmaineGordon.wordpress.com

And on her FB page
http://www.facebook.com/charmaine.gordon